Heart h
spun aro

The assailant was back. He'd apparently snuck up on Rose from behind while she was distracted with her call and clamped a hand over her mouth while pointing a gun at her head.

Henry reached for the pistol he'd kept tucked at the small of his back for most of his adult life, but of course it wasn't there. Now what? He was an experienced negotiator, but there was no opportunity for negotiation here. The gunman had the upper hand and Henry had...nothing. "Hey! Let her go!" Henry shouted, and then he charged the criminal because there was no other option.

The attacker's eyes rounded with surprise as Henry barreled toward him.

Rose grabbed the opportunity to twist her body and jab an elbow back into the attacker's gut.

Bang!

Henry's heart nearly stopped. Had Rose been shot?

"Rose!"

Jenna Night comes from a family of Southern-born natural storytellers. Her parents were avid readers and the house was always filled with books. No wonder she grew up wanting to tell her own stories. She's lived on both coasts but currently resides in the Inland Northwest, where she's astonished by the occasional glimpse of a moose, a herd of elk or a soaring eagle.

Books by Jenna Night

Love Inspired Suspense

Big Sky First Responders

Deadly Ranch Hideout
Witness Protection Ambush
Unsolved Montana Investigation
Dangerous Montana Inheritance

Range River Bounty Hunters

Abduction in the Dark
Fugitive Ambush
Mistaken Twin Target
Fugitive in Hiding

Rock Solid Bounty Hunters

Fugitive Chase
Hostage Pursuit
Cold Case Manhunt

Visit the Author Profile page at LoveInspired.com for more titles.

DANGEROUS MONTANA INHERITANCE

JENNA NIGHT

LOVE INSPIRED SUSPENSE
INSPIRATIONAL ROMANCE

LOVE INSPIRED® SUSPENSE
INSPIRATIONAL ROMANCE

ISBN-13: 978-1-335-95729-0

Recycling programs
for this product may
not exist in your area.

Dangerous Montana Inheritance

Love Inspired
22 Adelaide St. West, 41st Floor
Toronto, Ontario M5H 4E3, Canada
www.LoveInspired.com

Printed in Lithuania

MIX
Paper | Supporting
responsible forestry
FSC® C021394

The thief cometh not, but for to steal, and to kill, and to destroy: I am come that they might have life, and that they might have it more abundantly.
—*John* 10:10

To Esther Harris, who never gave up on my dream.
Thanks, Mom.

ONE

"I never thought I'd be involved in a murder," Rose Balfour said into the phone balanced between her ear and shoulder. "A murder *trial*," she quickly clarified.

"I never thought I'd be happily married with four kids by the time I was thirty," Rose's old friend from high school, Kendra, responded over the phone. "Life brings us plenty of surprises."

Indeed it did.

Rose glanced up at the sky filled with roiling deep purple clouds ready to dump rain on Cedar Lodge, Montana. She'd driven here directly from the regional airport after her two-week visit with Kendra and her family in Utah.

"You're there now, right?" Kendra asked. "You're at the house you inherited. What does it look like?"

Rose headed across the gravel driveway toward the front door. "It's not exactly the Boyd Mansion," she replied, referring to the beautiful historic home that had been a source of pride for the residents of Cedar Lodge until it burned down a little over a year ago. "This place is old and small. It's set on about a quarter acre of land in a section of town with a mixture of homes and businesses."

There was no reason for Rose to feel uneasy, but she did.

"I can't believe you were left a house by somebody you

didn't even know. This is so exciting," Kendra said. Her tone had the same enthusiasm she'd shown when Rose had been sitting across from her in Utah and reading aloud the email she'd just received about the house.

Rose had been stunned, at first. And then excited. But as the last few days had passed before she returned home, she'd grown uneasy.

The whole thing felt eerie.

The house had been bequeathed to her by Gabe Kraft, a loan shark who'd been murdered nearly a year ago. Tomorrow Rose would be giving testimony at Kraft's murder trial because she'd witnessed Kraft and the accused, Lance Preston, arguing the day before the murder occurred. She hadn't even clearly heard what they were saying, but the deputy prosecutor working the case had assured her during a pretrial video meeting yesterday that her testimony was important.

Apparently Kraft's family wanted the property and they'd kept Rose's inheritance secret until finally realizing that fighting the will was futile. The attorney who'd sent her the email had also sent her the code to unlock the front door. Curious, she'd decided to check out the property before heading to her condo on the other side of town.

Maybe that hadn't been such a great idea. Standing here now, she was a little bit afraid of what she might find inside. She should have brought someone with her to take her first look.

"It's all so mysterious," Kendra, a fan of true crime shows, enthused through the phone. "You didn't even know the guy."

Yes and no.

Rose's parents, who'd always been and still were financially irresponsible, had borrowed money from the now-deceased loan shark a few years back. Rose knew Gabe Kraft was a dangerous man. That's why she'd kept her eye on him after spotting him on the street and ended up witnessing the argument.

Rose hadn't explained that to Kendra because it would be embarrassing for her parents if people knew about the loan. While Kendra was a good friend, she was also an enthusiastic gossip.

"Are you inside the house yet?" Kendra asked impatiently.

Rose paused at the door, her stomach tying itself in knots. Could Kraft have left the door rigged with some kind of explosive device? She took a close look. Everything appeared normal. The loan shark had been murdered nearly a year ago; surely someone would have opened the front door to his house before now. She was being ridiculous.

"I'm about to go in."

Rose took a deep breath, punched in the code and then opened the door.

The stifling dead air was the first thing to catch her attention. After that, she noticed the living room was mostly set up as an office. There was a sofa and an easy chair, but there was also a large desk with a swivel chair and an old-school file cabinet.

"Well?" Kendra asked impatiently.

Rose set down her shoulder bag. She propped open the front door before opening a couple of windows to get some fresh air circulating.

"I guess this was the heart of his loan-sharking business," Rose replied.

On the other end of the call Rose heard a loud crash.

"I've got to go," Kendra said quickly. "Peter's climbed

onto the kitchen counter. Send some pics!" she added before disconnecting.

Rose shoved her phone into her pocket while looking around. "It's just a house," she said aloud, trying to shake off the nervous tension pulling her stomach muscles taut. "And Gabe Kraft is long gone."

Unease rippled across her skin as she stepped into the short hallway for a further look. She flipped a wall switch to chase away the shadows, but nothing happened. Her request to have the power restored apparently hadn't been processed yet. She pulled out her phone and turned on the flashlight app.

Continuing down the hallway, she shined the light into a bathroom to her right and a bedroom to her left. There was another bedroom up ahead and across from that the hallway made a sharp right turn, where she discovered a utility closet with a washer and dryer hookup.

And that was it. That was the whole house. The property was worth more than the building. But *why* had Gabe Kraft left it to her?

There was a narrow door ahead and she unfastened the lock and shoved it open to get a view of the side yard. Not much to look at out there. Just a narrow band of weeds, a chain-link fence and beyond that a field with a scattering of trees.

She shut the door and locked it, then headed back down the hallway, ready to go. Being here was giving her the creeps and she was growing increasingly anxious to leave.

As she walked down the hallway, she heard something disturbing the gravel outside and stopped to listen. The storm must have finally broken. It was probably rain falling.

After a couple more steps she heard someone talking outside. "She's not at her condo because she's here," an unfamiliar voice said quietly, the sound carrying through the partially open door and windows.

Rose stopped in her tracks.

"Copy that," the voice continued, "I know you want to talk to her first, so I'll keep her alive."

The hairs on the back of Rose's neck stood on end.

"Yeah, yeah," the voice continued impatiently. "Don't worry. She will *not* testify at the trial tomorrow. I guarantee it. I'll permanently silence her if I have to, but you've made it clear that's your second choice."

Rose's heart pounded and paralyzing fear made it impossible to move her feet. *Lord, protect me!*

The sound of footfalls coming up the wooden steps snapped her out of her frozen state and she spun around, racing to reach the turn in the hallway so she'd be out of view when the intruder stepped through the door.

"Hello!" the voice called out in a loud falsely friendly tone. "Rose Balfour, are you in here?"

Rose fumbled to unlock the back door as the creep moved toward her while calling out her name.

Her knees shook and she was lightheaded with fear when she finally got the lock unfastened and yanked open the door.

"Stop!" the assailant barked behind her, abandoning his attempt to sound friendly.

Rose ran out into the rain and toward the chain-link fence.

Bang!

The gunshot sent a stab of fear through her heart. She quickly scaled the barrier and dropped down on the other side. She fell to her knees upon landing, but pushed herself up and started running through the wild grass.

There were trees up ahead and she made a beeline for them, desperate to find cover before the attacker fired again. It wasn't a section of thick forest so it wouldn't be a place to try and hide for very long, but it was something.

An engine rumbled on the nearby road. Heading in that direction and flagging down someone to help her might be the better choice.

She spotted a heavy-duty pickup truck through the trees and veered toward it.

Bang!

Rose stumbled and then quickly regained her footing. That shot had been close. Rose was going to have to change tactics again. There was too much open ground between herself and the road. The gunman would likely take her out with his next round.

She shifted her trajectory, focused on making the most of the sparse cover of the trees. There had to be a house or a business up ahead, *something*, where she could get help.

The rain fell heavier and with the low dark clouds, it was hard to see ahead. She finally spotted something that she could tell wasn't another tree. She focused on the unrecognizable object, gasping for breath as she ran.

The object became more defined and she realized she was looking at racks of thick metal shelving holding objects of various shapes and sizes. Her toe caught on something and she was sent sprawling. As she scrambled back to her feet she noted a wooden railroad tie lying on the ground that seemed to be some sort of boundary marker. Beyond it were rows of small plants in containers.

She'd run to a plant nursery. There were fountains and statuary scattered around and sacks of fertilizer and potting soil, along with ceramic pots of varying sizes placed atop thick metal shelving.

"Help!" she tried to yell as loud as she could, but she was winded and her desperate call didn't have the volume she'd intended. She drew in a deep breath to call out again, but this time she sucked in rainwater and nearly choked on it.

Where were the shoppers and employees? Was the business not open yet since it was fairly early on a weekday? Or had they heard gunshots and hidden inside the main store or office, wherever that was located?

Pushing the sodden hair away from the front of her face, Rose looked around but couldn't see an office or anything similar because of all the shelving and objects in front of her. She couldn't just stand there, so she sprinted ahead past a row filled with plants and gardening tools, then past another lined with ceramic birdbaths. When she reached the next row, she turned and ran down it.

She heard the attacker trailing behind her, his footsteps slapping atop the mud and puddles of standing water. He hadn't reached the row she was in, and through gaps in the open shelving she caught glimpses of him moving.

Desperately looking for a place to hide, her attention snagged on a bottom shelf farther down the row holding a half dozen very large ceramic pots. Maybe she could climb onto the shelf and then wriggle behind the pots and get out of sight. Hopefully the gunman would rush by in a hurry trying to find her and wouldn't see her. It was the only thing she could think of to do, so she ran down the row, dropped to her hands and knees in the mud and then climbed onto the shelf. She crawled beside a terra-cotta pot that was at least three feet high and squeezed herself into a tight ball behind it, desperate to make herself invisible to the gunman as he approached. Having done all she could, she started praying.

Henry Walsh raced through the wet grass, weaving between the dripping branches of pine trees, hot on the heels of the woman he'd witnessed fleeing and the creep chasing after her.

Henry had been on his way back to his ranch after visiting a nearby flooring supply showroom when he'd seen the woman racing toward his truck as he drove by. He'd then heard a gunshot and watched her change directions as the shooter popped out from the cover of the trees and pursued her until they both disappeared from view.

He'd abruptly pulled his truck to the side of the road before leaping out and bolting after them, determined to help. Six years as an army ranger followed by seven years as a private security contractor had honed his skills and fueled his determination to help anyone in danger anytime he could.

While barreling forward, not having yet caught sight of them again, Henry reached for the gun tucked under the waistband at the small of his back. It wasn't there.

Of course not.

After thirteen years fighting vicious attackers of various sorts all around the world, he'd finally given up that life and returned home to Cedar Lodge where he'd figured he would no longer need a gun for personal protection.

So much for that.

With no time for second-guessing, he wrenched his attention back to the snapped tree branches and trampled wet grass in front of him. They made a trail that was easy to follow despite the limited visibility due to the rain. He could see they were headed toward the plant nursery.

Henry slowed as he reached the tree line, taking a quick visual survey of the multiple-acre display grounds of the business. If the woman had been able to keep her head and think clearly, she had a good chance of hiding until the gunman gave up on finding her. But panic was a real force that often caused people to make bad, sometimes fatal mistakes.

Henry headed for the endcaps where he'd be able to quickly look down each row as he searched for the woman. She might have bypassed the rows and headed for the office on the far side of the property, but even if he didn't find her, he might come across the shooter. And that would be okay with him. Henry had been in the position of having to disarm an attacker without having a gun of his own before. Not easy, but he knew he could do it.

Moving quickly and quietly, Henry looked down the first row, and seeing no one there, he continued on. There was no one in the second row, either, or the third, but looking down the fourth row he spotted the criminal, gun in hand, hurrying along while peering directly into the shelves. At least the creep had no situational awareness. He wasn't bothering to look around or behind him, which was a benefit for Henry.

Henry rushed to the next row, which was filled with an assortment of large ceramic pots. If he were trying to hide, this would be a likely place he'd choose. Using a ceramic fountain at the end of the row for cover, Henry scanned the lower shelves for movement. And then he saw her. She'd chosen a decent spot, having squeezed herself behind a large decorative pot. Henry could see sections of her curled-up torso from his angle. From the point of view of her pursuer, standing in front of the shelf and looking directly in, spotting her would be almost impossible.

The creep rounded the corner at the other end of the row where the woman was hiding and started walking in Henry's direction. Henry considered just attacking the thug, but once the surprised assailant started shooting, the bullets could go anywhere. Henry might manage to take cover and avoid them, but the woman could get shot. Better to wait and see if the creep just passed her by.

"Please don't move," Henry whispered to himself as the gunman began scanning the shelves. He could almost feel the woman's fear as if it were his own and his heart went out to her. He'd been in similar situations many times himself, anxious and trapped and feeling he could be killed at any moment.

Enough. Empathy was good to a point. But too much emotion crowded out logic and wasn't helpful at all.

Even so, his heart fell to his feet when he noticed the woman moving and realized she was climbing out of her hiding place, apparently afraid she was about to get caught. She slid from the shelf and raced in Henry's direction. She rushed toward him without seeing him. He reached out and grabbed her, placing his hand across her mouth before wrapping his other arm across her body. Then he quickly got them both hidden behind the fountain.

The woman fought against him and he didn't blame her one bit.

"I'm here to help," he whispered with his lips pressed to her ear.

She twisted a little more, and then finally turned to look up at him.

Henry found himself gazing into a face he hadn't seen in years. Since high school graduation, in fact. "Rose?" he asked in astonishment.

She stared back at him, wild-eyed. After a moment he saw that her panic had subsided and he moved his hand from her mouth. "Henry Walsh?" she said, sounding equally astonished. "Where did you come from?"

"I'll explain later," Henry whispered in reply.

Seeing Rose again and holding her in his arms was stirring up a doozy of an emotional storm. And that was a distraction he didn't need right now.

Henry angled himself so that Rose was behind him. "You start running for the business office." Henry turned to the side so she could hear him better while gesturing in the general direction she should go. "I'll get the situation under control here." He couldn't take the risk of the shooter picking up Rose's trail as she ran away. He would remain behind and keep the creep occupied.

"No!" Rose whispered back. "I'm not going to leave you."

Henry bit back a grim smile. Everything had always been an argument with Rose. *Everything.*

"You'll help me most by getting out of the way." He turned and gave her a gentle but determined shove. To his relief, she started running.

Henry crept silently down the row toward the assailant who was focused on the shelves in front of him. When Henry got close enough, he leaped on the gunman just as the criminal spotted him in his peripheral vision.

They both fell to the ground, grappling in the mud. The creep managed to kick the side of Henry's face, but the former ranger retaliated by grabbing hold of the gunman's ankle and twisting it. The assailant bent over in pain and Henry knocked the gun from the guy's hand before he could get off a shot.

The criminal rolled over and recovered his weapon before Henry could get to it.

Approaching sirens wailed in the distance.

By now Henry was up and balanced on the balls of his feet, his gaze locked on the gun, readying himself to leap on the attacker again and get the weapon before the criminal could use it. A permanent injury to Henry's shoulder meant his hand-to-hand combat skills weren't as top-notch as they once were, but he was confident they were good enough to deal with this creep.

The gunman glanced toward the approaching sirens and began to back away. He fired a wild shot in Henry's direction before turning and running to the end of the row and then disappearing from view.

Instinct screamed at Henry to go after the shooter, but his fear for Rose's safety outweighed that impulse. Was the shooter going to try to get away before the cops arrived, or did he intend to find Rose and finish what he'd set out to do? Henry had to make sure Rose was all right.

He ran toward the nursery's office several yards away, where a wide-eyed young man in an employee vest stared at him through the glass door. Henry spotted Rose inside the office alongside a couple of other employees. She was gesturing wildly, likely demanding the guy let Henry in. The young man opened the door for Henry to slip inside and then slammed it shut behind him and locked it.

"We heard gunfire and called the cops," the man said.

Henry nodded before turning to Rose, relief flooding his body that she was all right. "You okay?" he asked, just in case she had an injury that he didn't see.

"I'm fine," she responded, though the words sounded shaky. She was pale, shivering, rain-soaked and appeared ready to burst into tears.

Henry slid off his jacket and held it out to her. She shook her head and refused to take it. "Please," he said.

She took it and slipped it on. "Thank you."

"What happened?" Henry asked. "Who was that guy? Why was he after you?"

She drew in a shaky breath. "I'm supposed to testify in

the Gabe Kraft murder trial tomorrow." When Henry didn't respond right away, she frowned. "It's been in the news."

"Okay," Henry said. He wasn't exactly up-to-date on local happenings.

"I don't know who that man was who tried to kill me." Rose's voice caught. "I overheard him on his phone telling somebody that he'd grab me or kill me, but either way he'd make sure I didn't testify."

Police cars pulled up in front of the office.

Rose swiped at the tears that began rolling down her cheeks.

Henry wasn't sure how to respond to her display of emotions, which wasn't unusual for him.

He shifted his gaze to the front door as his old friend Officer Kris Volker approached and the clerk hurried over to unfasten the lock. Then Henry turned his attention back to Rose.

Without needing any further details, Henry could see that Rose needed someone to protect her, and he had the experience to do it.

But would she let him?

TWO

Wearing Henry Walsh's jacket felt like having his noticeably muscular arms wrapped around her, and Rose wasn't sure how she felt about that.

This was the guy who had teased her through all four years of high school. Nothing especially mean, just annoying comments about her glasses or her consistent placement on the honor roll or how much time she spent studying and working in the library. She'd rarely had an actual conversation with him because he was so hardheaded that it was impossible to discuss anything without getting into an argument.

But just now, over a dozen years since she'd last seen him, he'd appeared from out of nowhere and saved her life. She was grateful, and that was normal enough. The disconcerting thing was the nervous fluttering in the pit of her stomach. Henry had thrown himself into the middle of a potentially deadly situation like some kind of superhero, and on top of that, the guy had become flat-out handsome over the years. The cocky, smart-aleck grin he used to wear all the time was gone. Now Rose could see compassion in his dark brown eyes, which were bracketed by lines marking the passage of time, and a determined set to his lips and jawline that showed nothing of the mockery that used to be his go-to reaction to everything.

With a start, she realized she'd been staring at him while pondering the situation and she looked away. A moment later she realized that he had been staring at her, too, and her cheeks warmed.

The warmth didn't last long, though, as the realization of what might have happened if Henry hadn't shown up began to sink in. If it weren't for Henry, her life could have been over by now.

"Thank you for helping me," she said, shifting her gaze back to him. His inky-black hair was cut in a short military style and there was a spray of small white scars across his heavily tanned face. Combat injuries, maybe? She'd heard that he'd gone into the military right after high school. And later, after his three high school buddies who'd also enlisted after graduation had completed their service and returned home, Henry had stayed overseas working for a private security company. Rose had never heard any specific details about what that more recent job involved.

Henry replied to her expression of gratitude with a slight nod. "Glad to be of assistance, but it looked to me like you were handling things pretty well on your own."

Rose blinked in surprise. A *humble* response from big-mouth braggard Henry Walsh? That was unheard of. But they'd both had time to do some growing up. Henry's parents had been drug-dealing criminals, everybody knew about it, and that had to have been stressful and embarrassing for Henry. As a teenager, Rose hadn't understood that he was acting out because of an unstable home life. As an adult, she now realized he'd been under a lot of pressure back then and had likely been handling a rough situation as best he could.

Her own homelife had had its own measure of instability. Both her parents had rejected the corporate lifestyle they'd grown up around in southern California and moved to Montana after getting married to pursue a more down-to-earth lifestyle. The result had been years of constant job changes and financial insecurity as her mom and dad based many of their decisions on the impulse or emotion of the moment. Once Rose was old enough to understand what was happening, she'd become determined to do things differently. The result, admittedly, was a tendency to be hyper-organized and easily frustrated with anyone who seemed to be slacking off and just floating through life. Which was how Henry had often seemed to her.

So what had caused them to cross paths today in such an extreme way?

"Are you a cop now?" Rose asked, trying to figure out the specific event that had sent him to her rescue. His three best friends in high school had all taken public service jobs after their time in the military, so maybe Henry had decided to do the same thing and he was undercover or off-duty or something. Kris Volker, who was just now walking through the door, had become a city cop. Cole Webb was a paramedic and Dylan Ruiz was a deputy sheriff.

Henry shook his head at her question. "Just happened to be in the neighborhood. I heard gunshots, then saw you running and that creep chasing after you. Well, I didn't realize it was *you* that was running, but I saw a woman who obviously needed some help. Figured I'd jump in and do whatever I could."

Rose's stomach knotted as her thoughts returned to the fear coursing through her as she'd tried to get out of the house and then escape the pursuing gunman.

When Henry had first grabbed her, she'd thought her life

was over. And then, slowly, she'd begun to realize she was in the arms of a man who was trying to help her.

"You two all right?" Officer Kris Volker asked as he stepped up to them.

Rose wasn't close friends with Kris, but they'd been acquaintances since high school. "I'm fine." She looked past Kris at two more cop cars pulling up outside.

"I'm A-okay," Henry added. "In case you were worried about *me*."

Kris ignored his old friend and said to Rose, "Tell me what happened."

She gave him a quick summary, ending with, "I assume the creep originally drove to the house and parked there, so he probably ran back to get his vehicle and drive away."

"Not sure how fast he's running," Henry said quietly. "I twisted his ankle pretty good."

Kris keyed his radio mic to relay the information and the cop cars outside sped off. "So what does the perp look like?"

"Average height," Rose said. "Blond, collar-length hair. Blue eyes. Late thirties, I'd say, and skinny. And he's wearing a gray jacket and jeans."

Kris sent out the additional information over his radio. Then he turned to the store clerk who seemed to be in charge. "I'll need to see your security video for the grounds so I can get an image of the perp."

The clerk shook his head. "We only have cameras in here where we've got the cash registers and by the front and rear entrances for the sake of employee security. Nothing outside."

Rose's phone chimed and she reached into her pocket to look at the screen. "It's a text from Deputy Prosecutor

Nate Sloane confirming that I've returned from Utah and that I'll be in court to give testimony tomorrow morning."

"The judge for that case will want to know about this attack," Kris said. "She might decide to suspend the proceedings until you've had time to recover from what you've been through. Chief Ellis is going to want to talk to you, too. Let me get word to the courthouse about this so they can inform the judge and then I'll have you and Henry come with me to the police station."

"Okay." Now that the adrenaline spike had bottomed out, Rose's head was starting to pound. She hoped she'd be able to get some type of pain reliever and a cup of coffee when they got to the station.

After that, she wasn't sure what she would do. The attacker and whoever he was talking with on the phone knew about her condo so she wouldn't feel safe going home. She was also afraid if she stayed with her parents or friends, she would put them in danger. Maybe she'd check into one of the B and Bs on the banks of the Meadowlark River.

All she wanted to do as soon as she was finished at the police station was go someplace where she could get some rest and feel safe. She was trying to appear calm around Henry and Kris, but the truth was with the shooter running loose in town, she was very much afraid.

In the conference room at the Cedar Lodge police station Henry did his best not to get caught gazing at Rose while she answered Kris Volker's questions for his report. Henry had already given his statement. Getting Rose's recounting of the events entered into the database was taking longer since she obviously had more information to offer.

Henry had always thought Rose Balfour was pretty, with sable-colored hair and hazel eyes, but back in high school she'd worn glasses and she didn't have them on now. He missed them. The black plastic frames had suited her sharp features. He'd liked her back in school, but he knew a straight-edge girl like her would never be interested in a guy from a shady family like him so he'd gone overboard trying to make it appear as if he weren't interested. He'd wanted to save himself the embarrassment of rejection.

Of course he didn't understand that at the time. It was one of the many things he figured out about himself later, when he got out of town. He'd surrounded himself with quality people during his stint in the military, and in the course of doing that found a faith that had given him the strength to face and figure out some of the emotional garbage that had been weighing him down for a while.

When Rose, Henry and Kris had first sat down at the conference table, Rose had turned to Henry with that level gaze of hers that he'd interpreted as judgmental back in high school. But then he'd seen nearly everybody in town as judgmental when he was a kid whose parents were routinely too drunk or stoned to notice that he'd been staying at his friend Kris Volker's ranch for several days and hadn't been home in nearly a week.

But now, while occasionally gazing at her as she spoke with Kris, he'd realized this was the expression she wore when she was thinking things through. She read books and pondered what was in them and always got good grades, and Henry had found that fascinating, since there was nothing like that going on at his house when he was a teenager.

It bugged Henry that he still cared what Rose thought of him. Maybe he'd risen in her estimation after he helped her out earlier today, but he wasn't going to put himself in the position of finding out.

He'd come back to Cedar Lodge to repair the ranch he'd

inherited so that he could sell it for a good price, and then he'd be gone. Cedar Lodge was a quaint town in a beautiful setting, but he'd said goodbye to living here. Withstanding the scorn of people who knew he was the son of self-absorbed parents who made their living off people in the throes of addiction wasn't something he would put himself through. He had plenty of friends he'd served with offering him jobs working corporate security within the US. He had other options, other places where he could live.

Kris was tapping at the keyboard attachment to his tablet and Rose was sipping her coffee when Chief Ellis entered the conference room carrying a laptop.

"How are you holding up?" the chief asked Rose.

"A lot better now that I have this." She gestured at her coffee cup.

"Good." He turned to Henry. "Not surprised to find you in the center of trouble."

Meant as good-natured ribbing, of course, but still a sore spot for Henry even after all the years he'd spent away from Cedar Lodge building a work history and reputation he was proud of. He stole another glance at Rose. No doubt she still thought of him as the guy with the shady background despite the fact that he'd never indulged in criminal behavior himself.

He looked away. It didn't matter how pretty Rose was. Or how much he admired the courage she'd shown while getting chased by that creep. They weren't going to be forming any kind of friendship, much less anything beyond that. Throughout his high school years, Henry had compulsively tried to show people he was a funny, friendly guy and not some sort of degenerate. He'd finally been able to put that compulsion behind him, and he was not going back to trying to convince anybody in town—Rose included—that he was a decent person.

Henry focused his attention on the police chief. Henry and Ellis had crossed paths many times back when Ellis had still been a patrolman and Henry's parents were getting picked up by the cops time after time. Fortunately, then-patrolman Ellis had recognized the tough situation Henry was in and offered him compassion along with helpful advice on occasion since the situation hadn't quite met the threshold where child protective services would have taken custody of Henry. Upon Henry's return to town, the two of them had reconnected at a barbecue hosted by Kris Volker and his wife, Monica, at their family ranch.

"What's the next step?" Henry asked. "I'll do anything I can to help you catch this guy."

"I'm waiting to hear back from Judge Markham," the chief said as he took a seat. He turned to Rose. "She requested a video chat with you, and I expect her to call any minute. Maybe she'll have some idea who the assailant is. Could be there are some behind-the-scenes situations about the case that would shine a light on today's attack."

"I hope you can catch the shooter quickly," Rose said, running her finger along the side of her coffee cup. "Maybe when you catch him you can figure out who he was talking to on the phone and get that guy, too."

Seeing Rose downcast and fearful stoked the simmering frustration in Henry's gut. Rose was a decent person, he knew that, and he wanted to personally bring the jerk who'd attacked her to justice and find that loser's accomplice as well. Henry wasn't a cop, so he was limited in what he could do. But he would do all he could to make her world safe again.

Ellis crossed his arms and leaned back in his chair. "Speaking of behind-the-scenes situations, talk to me about this house you inherited and why a dangerous loan shark would bequeath it to you."

"Rose?" Her name escaped Henry's lips as his heart stilled in his chest. Straight-arrow Rose Balfour was involved with a loan shark? How could that be? Granted, nobody was perfect and it wasn't fair to put that kind of pressure on anyone. But in his mind Rose had been someone who had her life completely put together.

"I don't know why Gabe Kraft left me that stupid house," she snapped, her eyes flashing with irritation. "And now I don't want it."

"But why you?" Ellis pressed.

Yeah, Rose, why you? A sour feeling of jealousy stirred within Henry. It was ridiculous, given that he hadn't seen Rose in over a dozen years, and even back in the day they'd had no real friendship or romantic connection. He just couldn't stand the thought that she might have somehow been manipulated or conned into a relationship with a criminal.

Rose drained her paper coffee cup and then set it on the table with more force than was necessary, leaving it slightly crumpled. "Look, my only connection with Gabe Kraft is that my parents borrowed money from him, one time, five years ago."

Wait, *what?* Rose's parents borrowed money from a loan shark? Henry's shoulders slumped as it occurred to him that Rose might have had upsetting things going on in her home life back when they were teenagers that he'd known nothing about. Situations that no one even suspected, possibly. Because the only thing anyone saw was the overachiever straight-A student. There was no way his clueless teenage self could have picked up on anything as subtle as that, but he still wanted to kick himself for being so oblivious.

"Gabe Kraft tried to cheat my parents," Rose continued,

her voice having grown stronger. She lifted her chin. "I was horrified when I found out they'd taken out the loan. But then I asked them for the details and began documentation of their cash payments to him, helping with that as much as I could, to get the whole thing taken care of and over with as efficiently as possible. At the end, he showed up at their house and claimed they still owed him money. They called me and I came over and showed him my documentation that they had paid him everything they owed."

Henry couldn't help smiling. Having detailed information and shoving it in the face of the loan shark sounded exactly like the Rose he'd known and possibly had a crush on.

"Kraft was surprised and laughed it off," Rose continued. "I took the chance that he thought of himself as some kind of businessman and said if he kept it up I'd make sure word got out and desperate people would look elsewhere to get the money they needed. And you know what? It actually worked. He left my parents alone after that."

Henry's shoulders straightened back up. It wasn't his place to feel proud of Rose, but he did.

"That's it," Rose said. "The extent of any contact I had with him. If there was anything else, I'd tell you because I don't want to get killed."

Ellis nodded, his stony expression not revealing whether he believed her or not. "We're going to do everything we can to catch the bad guys and get this wrapped up so you don't have to worry about that."

Did Henry believe Rose? That she had no relationship with Gabe Kraft other than what she'd just described? He did.

"The mug shots I requested are ready," Kris said. He'd been quietly listening and occasionally glancing at his tablet for the last several minutes. "I need you guys to take a look at these." He slid the device across the table toward

Rose and Henry. "These are some local criminals known for violence who match the physical description you gave," he said. "Tell me if any of them look all familiar."

They swiped through but Henry didn't see the attacker. Rose came to the same conclusion.

"It's okay," Kris told Rose reassuringly. "We're just getting started. We'll find the perp."

The chief's laptop chimed and he tapped it to connect with the incoming video call. "Good morning, Your Honor."

Was it really still morning? Henry glanced at the wall clock showing it was close to noon. He turned his attention back to the laptop the chief had positioned so that all of them could see the screen. Judge Markham asked about Rose's well-being and then quickly moved on to a series of questions as she was obviously trying to ferret out whether Rose knew the attacker or if anyone else had threatened Rose regarding her testimony.

"Will you be prepared to testify tomorrow or shall I postpone the trial?"

"I want to get this over with as quickly as possible," Rose answered. "After I've given my testimony, there'll be no reason for the attacker and whoever he's working with to try again to kidnap or kill me."

"All right." The judge looked toward the police chief. "I anticipate that Ms. Balfour will be kept safe until she can arrive in court."

Ellis nodded. "We'll take care of that."

"Good."

The judge disconnected and Ellis turned to Rose. "We'll find a place for you to stay tonight and stage a cop outside the door."

"Let me protect her," Henry said.

Rose stared at him.

"I have extensive experience in confronting hostile combatants," Henry continued, shifting his attention to Rose. "My grandma left me her ranch outside of town when she passed away a few years ago. We've got several dogs up there and if someone approaches the house, they let us know about it."

"Us?" Rose asked.

"My cousin and his wife live on the property with me. They're helping me with repairs before I sell it. I don't plan to stay around town for very long."

That should make it clear that he wasn't hitting on her and that he was just suggesting he protect her because it was something he could do.

"You should take him up on his offer," Kris told Rose.

Rose studied Henry for a moment as she considered.

"If you're not comfortable with that arrangement, we can figure out something else," Chief Ellis said as he closed his laptop and stood. "But for what it's worth, I think staying at the ranch for the night is a good idea."

"Okay." Rose turned to Henry. "Thank you for your offer, and I accept. But first I want to go back to Kraft's house and get my car and then I'll follow you to your ranch."

"All right, let's go." As Henry got to his feet, he did his best to ignore the little frisson of nerves in the pit of his stomach. Admittedly he was a little uneasy about spending more time with Rose despite his determination to not even consider any kind of continuing connection with her. Good thing Rose would give her testimony in court tomorrow and things would be wrapped up. After that, she should be safe and Henry could go back to figuring out his future away from Cedar Lodge.

* * *

"Let's make this quick," Henry said to Rose as they drove up to Gabe Kraft's house.

"Okay."

From the corner of his eye, he could see her nervously chewing her bottom lip and holding her hands clasped tightly in her lap.

Henry imagined she was mentally rehashing what had happened to her earlier. "We can just go to the ranch and come back for your car later, if you want."

"No, I want to do this." Rose squared her shoulders. "I'm going to need my car tomorrow." She turned to Henry. "And I want to get back to feeling normal as quicky as possible."

"Understood." Admiration for her courage tempted Henry to gaze at her a little bit longer, but he didn't want to make her uncomfortable so he turned away and surveyed their surroundings instead. There were trees scattered around along with a few clumps of wild grass and some small outbuildings toward the backyard and on neighboring properties. Old habits had him already picking out places where a shooter could potentially hide.

Rose opened her door and slid out. Henry got out of the truck to go with her, even though she was only walking to her car.

"I want to make sure the doors of the house are locked before we go." She offered Henry a self-conscious smile that tugged at his heart. "Maybe Gabe Kraft left me the house because of something inside. I'd like to have the chance to look for it before a thief can get in and potentially take it."

Henry didn't want to linger here, but he didn't argue. It was her call. "All right." He stepped ahead of her at the front door. "But let me go in first." He hadn't seen or heard any sign of movement in the house, but he wasn't taking any chances.

The door was unlocked and Henry held it open while scanning the shadowy interior of the house. It was quiet, and after a few moments he indicated to Rose that the scene appeared safe for entry. They headed for the back of the house where Rose locked the door. She then made certain all the windows were closed and locked before they returned to secure the front door and then stepped back outside.

Rose's phone pinged and she glanced at the screen. "It's work. Let me make a quick call before we go."

"Sure." Since she was understandably still rattled and nervous, Henry figured the added distraction of a phone call while driving wouldn't be safe. He watched her take a couple of steps away from him as she placed her call and Henry moved a short distance away to give her added privacy.

Near one of the house's front windows he spotted trampled grass where somebody—likely the assailant—had tried peeking inside. Henry was checking to see which direction the tracks originated from when he heard a muffled scream. Heart hammering in his chest, he spun around.

The assailant was back. He'd apparently snuck up on Rose from behind while she was distracted with her call and clamped a hand over her mouth while pointing a gun at her head.

Henry reached for the pistol he'd kept tucked at the small of his back for most of his adult life, but of course, as had been the case during the attack earlier in the day, it wasn't there. Now what? He was an experienced negotiator, but there was no opportunity for negotiation here. The gunman had the upper hand and Henry had…nothing. "Hey! Let her go!" Henry shouted and then he charged the criminal because there was no other option.

The attacker's eyes rounded with surprise as Henry barreled toward him.

Rose grabbed the opportunity to twist her body and jab an elbow back into the attacker's gut.

Bang!

Henry's heart nearly stopped. Had Rose been shot?

"Rose!"

"Henry!" she screamed in response, having wrenched her mouth away from the attacker's hand.

Henry kept charging, praying Rose wouldn't be hurt as he leaped forward and knocked both Rose and the assailant to the ground in an attempt to get the gun away from the attacker.

Rose bit and kicked at the guy at the same time that Henry wrestled with him. Henry managed to twist the gun from the assailant's hand and then quickly got to his feet, his gaze and the weapon both focused on the criminal who was now trying to stand. For all Henry knew, the assailant could have a second weapon so Henry remained wary.

"Are you hurt?" Henry called to Rose. "Were you shot?" He risked a quick glance at her, desperate to know she was all right.

"I'm okay," Rose replied in a shaky voice.

She didn't appear to be wounded. The bullet must have missed her. *Thank You, Lord.*

In the next instant Henry saw the flash of a knife blade in his peripheral vision. He ducked and spun out of reach just as the criminal's arm swung down and the tip of the knife caught on the side of Henry's shirt and cut through it. The attacker quickly sidestepped so that he was between Henry and Rose, with his knife extended toward Henry and positioned for another attack. With Rose in the line of fire, Henry didn't dare take a shot.

Torn between the instinct to stay close to Rose to protect her and the tactical option of moving back to draw the creep farther away from her, Henry locked his gaze on the knife blade while considering his next move.

"Help!" Rose called out.

Afraid a second assailant had appeared, Henry jerked his attention back in her direction as she added, "We're under attack at the Kraft house!" She was shouting into her phone and moving away from the attacker.

Henry focused on the creep again, prepared to fire at him if he had to now that Rose was a safe distance away. All Henry had to do was prevent the attacker from fleeing before the cops rolled up, which should be soon since he could already hear the wailing of an approaching siren.

Finally they could get some answers and find out who was behind all of this.

"Who are you working for?" Henry demanded of the thug.

The creep's calculating gaze flickered toward the siren sound of the approaching cop car before returning to Henry. Then he looked toward Rose as she continued to update the dispatcher while remaining out of the criminal's reach.

After spitting out a string of curses, the assailant spun around and ran.

"Stop!" Henry yelled, but the guy kept going until he leaped over a section of chain-link fence onto the neighbor's property and shortly after that disappeared from view.

Henry couldn't get a clear shot at the fleeing man, and he didn't want to risk accidentally injuring a civilian who might hear the altercation and come out to see what was happening. Frustrated, he whirled around to tell Rose to update the cops on the direction the gunman was escaping. But then he realized she was already doing that.

He strode over to her. "You certain you're all right?" he asked. "And that jerk didn't hurt you?" Maybe she had been injured but adrenaline had kept her from feeling any pain.

"Yeah, I'm sure."

Physically she might be okay. But Henry could see in her eyes that this second attack had taken an emotional toll. He leaned down and pressed his forehead to hers for a moment, just to remind her that she wasn't in this dangerous situation alone. That he was here for her.

Two police cars shot past on the road, sirens wailing, as they headed in the direction the assailant had fled. A third cop car rolled up the driveway toward Henry and Rose. Hopefully the perp would quickly be caught. But even then, the situation probably wouldn't be resolved. Whoever had sent the criminal to silence Rose would likely send someone else to finish the job.

Rose would not allow herself to get interested in Henry Walsh no matter how intriguing the man was. She'd felt too rattled to drive after the second attack, so she'd just grabbed her suitcase and left her car at Kraft's house for the time being. The little electric *zing* she felt sitting beside Henry in the cab of his pickup truck as he drove her to his ranch was just the residual effect of having him save her life twice in a single day. That was all. And even if she did feel a slight attraction to him, so what? The heroic "glow" surrounding the man would wear off in a few hours or days at most and after that he would go back to being teasing, annoying Henry Walsh. A very brave and physically fit Henry Walsh, she couldn't deny.

Henry turned off the county highway onto a narrow

winding road that took them up the flank of Grizzly Mountain and through twisting miles of dense shadowy forest. The second attack had necessitated a second trip to the police station and by the time they'd left, it was well past noon. "What exactly did your family raise up here?" Rose asked. "This is some rough terrain."

"Nothing recently. But back in the day they raised cattle."

They hit a rut in the road and Rose grabbed the door handle for stability until things smoothed out again.

"My parents lived in town," he added. "My grandma stayed up here and boarded horses until taking care of them got to be too much for her. I came up to see her as often as I could. She was a woman of faith, which was something I appreciated, though it took a while for me to become a believer. It was largely because of her that I figured out there were lots of options in life and that the hard-partying, criminal lifestyle of my parents was not the way to go."

He cleared his throat and looked out the side window.

Rose's heart ached with sympathy. If she knew him better, she would have reached out to put her hand on his arm to let him know she was moved by what he'd just told her. But she didn't know him that well.

Being as subtle as possible, she glanced at him from the corner of her eye. His jaw was set, his shoulders looked tense and he continued to scan their surroundings and check his rearview mirror at regular intervals. It seemed highly unlikely someone would spring out at them from the thick forest on the sides of the narrow road. More likely, his hypervigilance was habit. This was a tough man who'd been through some tough times. This wasn't the class clown she'd known when they were kids.

What did he think of her? she wondered. Or did he even

think of her at all, beyond her being another person he could help defend in a dangerous world?

They rounded a corner and the forest gave way to open land. Barking dogs ran at them from several directions. She counted four of them, three large canines while the fourth was a long-haired Chihuahua desperately trying to catch up with the others. All of them were wagging their tails.

Rose took note of a moderate-size ranch house that looked old and had definitely seen better days. Farther on, she spotted a newish-looking pole barn and solidly built stables. A mixture of structures looked on the verge of falling apart, while others, like the house and stables, were being refurbished.

Henry pulled to a stop and they got out of the truck. The dogs gave them both a friendly greeting and Rose petted each of them in return.

The front door swung open and a man and woman who appeared to be in their mid-twenties strode out. "Did you at least get the flooring picked out before you went looking for trouble?" the man demanded of Henry with mock disappointment.

"The comedian is my cousin, Bennie," Henry said to Rose. "And beside him is his wife, Vivien."

Bennie looked like a shorter, slightly chubbier version of Henry. Vivien was taller than her husband with freckles and bright red hair.

After greetings were exchanged, Vivien stepped up to usher Rose into the ranch house. "I know it looks a little rough on the outside, but inside it's very clean."

"Thanks," Rose said. "I appreciate you letting a stranger into your home."

"It's Henry's house, not mine," Vivien said with a smile. "And I have to admit, I've been excited to meet you since we got the call telling us he was bringing you up here. I don't think he's ever brought a woman to the ranch."

Rose didn't know how to respond to that so she just kept her mouth shut. Henry had invited her here to keep her safe for one night and then it would all be over. There was no reason for the delighted little thrill fluttering in her stomach.

Henry grabbed Rose's suitcase from his truck and everyone headed for the front door. Rose reached out to pet a fat orange tabby cat sprawled across a rocking chair on the porch.

"That's Melvin," Henry said.

The furry feline dropped its head slightly so Rose could better reach the spots behind its ears.

What a strange day this had been and it was only half over, Rose thought as she reached the threshold of the house. But she had come through it unscathed and Henry Walsh had, too.

Henry Walsh. She shook her head, still a bit unsettled at having run into him after all these years. Because back in the day, even though he had annoyed Rose endlessly, there had still been a part of her that found him a little bit cute. He wasn't exactly cute now, as a thirty-one-year-old man. But he was definitely *something.*

Thank You, Lord, for protecting us today.

Now all she had to do was get to the courthouse safely tomorrow, give her testimony and all this danger and drama would be over.

That was what she wanted to believe. But given the frightening determination of the attacker, Rose wasn't certain it was true.

THREE

Henry took a sip of coffee the following morning in the ranch kitchen, determined to feel wide-awake.

Yesterday afternoon had been blessedly quiet after Rose had been installed in the extra bedroom, nicely prepared for her by Viv, and work on the ranch had settled into its normal routine. Viv and Bennie had resumed thinning the wild blackberry vines that had taken over the kitchen garden while Henry had worked on white rail fencing along the meadow near the front of the house where he could see anyone who might approach.

After settling in Rose had come out to the front porch to sit and visit Melvin the cat while making a couple of phone calls. After that she'd picked out something from the box of used paperbacks Bennie had recently bought and spent some time reading.

Having been through some traumatic experiences himself, Henry knew what she was feeling. Or thought he did. She'd nearly been killed. Twice. Her perception of the world and her place in it had likely radically changed. There was nothing like the first experience of having someone shoot at you with the intent to kill to remind you of how fragile life was.

Reading a good book was one way to shove all those

feelings of fear and anxiety aside for a short while until you felt better able to deal with them.

More than once Henry had been tempted to put down his hammer and go up to the porch to see if she wanted to talk about the attacks. But he hadn't done it. He and Rose weren't friends. After all this time they barely knew each other, and he didn't feel it was his place to intrude on her thoughts. A quiet laugh escaped him as he considered his thoughtfulness yesterday. The old Henry Walsh would have barreled up to talk to Rose as soon as the thought crossed his mind, without consideration for whether she wanted him to or not.

Life experience and the passage of time had changed Henry. It still wasn't clear to him how those same things might have changed Rose. She hadn't been talkative at dinner last night or a short while ago at breakfast this morning. And he supposed he wouldn't ever know how she'd changed, because Rose had just gone to grab her handbag and suitcase from her bedroom so they could leave for the courthouse. Once he got her there safely, that would likely be the last he'd see of her.

"Okay, I'm ready to go," Rose called out as she rolled her suitcase to the front door and waited for Henry.

She was wearing gray slacks and a royal blue sweater and she'd pulled her sable hair into a high ponytail. Henry had bit back a smile when she showed up at the breakfast table earlier wearing black-framed glasses similar to what she'd worn in high school. He could easily remember her happily reshelving library books back when they were both teenagers, or scurrying over to the computers and closing the tabs left open by students who hadn't cleared the screen when they were finished working.

"Hopefully, I won't get shot at again," Rose joked nervously, and a knot of anger formed in the pit of Henry's stomach over what she'd been forced to go through yesterday and the fact that the attacker still hadn't been captured. Rose Balfour should not have to live in fear.

"I'll let Kris know we're leaving." Henry pulled his phone from his pocket and keyed a quick message as they left the ranch house. "He's planning to meet up with us at the edge of town and give us an escort to the courthouse. We'll make sure you get inside safely so you can give your testimony and then this will all be over."

He put in the effort to make sure his words sounded neutral. The stupid little pang of sadness or regret or whatever it was he felt over saying a final goodbye to Rose was ridiculous and just some pathetic wisp of nostalgia. There was no possibility of Henry forming a friendship—or anything else—with Rose. He had plans to fix up the ranch, sell it and then leave town to start a new career somewhere else. Rose, on the other hand, appeared to be happily settled in Cedar Lodge.

It was a beautiful town, but Henry couldn't stay in a place where people still thought of him as some kind of social misfit because of his parents. Didn't matter that his mom and dad had divorced and both left Cedar Lodge years ago. People in small towns had long memories.

They got in the truck and he started the engine.

"So, I guess you've had a lot of experience trying not to get shot," Rose said in a tone that strained at sounding lighthearted.

"I've been fired at a few times," Henry said. His former careers as a ranger and private contractor specializing in hostage negotiation and rescue weren't exactly a lighthearted conversational topic for him. Beyond that, he had no desire to relate stories that might sound as if he were trying to present himself as some kind of hero.

"I heard you went into the army," Rose prompted. "After that, I heard you went into private security contract work, but I'm not exactly sure what that means."

"You've been keeping up on me?" Henry raised his eyebrows before turning and giving her a wink. "Gotta say I'm flattered."

Rose made a familiar scoffing sound and crossed her arms over her chest. "Hardly!"

Henry enjoyed her indignant reaction. Maybe he hadn't grown up all that much, after all.

"I just happened to overhear people talking about you," she added defensively.

Henry didn't bother to hide his smile. It sounded as if Rose was at least a little bit interested in him and that made Henry happy.

His boyish glee was short-lived, though. As they drew near to the edge of the ranch property, he needed to focus on their surroundings in anticipation of trouble. He didn't need to be flirting with Rose.

They reached the intersection with the four-lane highway and Henry's senses ramped up to full alert. He hadn't survived in hostile environments over the years by discounting the possibility of danger in any situation. "I specialized in international hostage rescue and negotiation," he finally said. "What have you been doing over the last dozen years?"

"Nothing nearly as exciting as that," Rose said after a slight hesitation. "I left for Missoula to go to college. My parents got into some financial hot water so I dropped out and came back to help them. Later, I tried resuming my college education, but my parents had trouble yet again, so once more I had to drop out and that was the end of it. I never went back."

One thing Henry could say about his own parents—they didn't do a lot for him, but they didn't ask for much from him, either. Except when Grandma Willa had left him the ranch, and his dad had been mad about that. He'd wanted Henry to sign it over to him. Henry hadn't done it.

"Long story short, I got a series of jobs in town and now I'm the office manager for an insurance agency," Rose continued. "I like my job. I've made enough to buy my own home and travel a little." She signed deeply. "It may sound like I'm ungrateful, but I'm kind of bored with it all. I went to visit my friend in Utah because I'm thinking of moving there and giving college a try one more time."

"What do you want to study?"

"Business administration."

Henry glanced over at her and she shrugged.

"I've always had a knack for dealing with details and I like keeping things organized."

"That's true," Henry said with a laugh. He'd seen evidence of that.

"Did you ever get married?" Henry asked a moment later. She could be married right now for all he knew. He hadn't seen a ring on her finger and she hadn't mentioned a husband, but that didn't prove she was single.

"No," she said.

"Why not?" Probably a dumb question, but Rose was a smart beautiful woman. "Are you not interested in getting married?"

"Why? Are you asking me to marry *you*?" she teased.

"I deserved that," Henry said before laughing. This was the Rose he knew, able to give as good as she got.

"I've had a couple of relationships that I thought might

become serious," Rose said, "but they ended up fizzling out. What about you?"

"I never even came close. My career wasn't conducive to quality relationships, never mind a marriage."

"Sounds like it would have been a challenge," Rose agreed.

In the past it would have been. But his life had recently changed.

Six months ago Henry had ventured into an ambush while trying to track down a group of recently relocated hostages, and the injuries that resulted had put him in the hospital for an extended stay. The attack ultimately derailed his career since his shoulder had ended up with a permanently limited range of motion. He could still put up a good fight if he needed to, but his body hadn't completely returned to the capacity it had been at before the attack.

While he was laid up, he'd spent more time reflecting on his life than he was normally comfortable with. It was the first time the fact that he didn't have a family of his own struck him as being a sad situation. Marriage and children weren't exactly on his radar right now, but he could see it happening in the future. The distant future. Not while living in Cedar Lodge.

They approached the edge of town and Henry spotted Kris Volker in a city police patrol car. Their mutual friend, Deputy Dylan Ruiz, was in a county sheriff's patrol car behind him. Both cops were in pullouts by the side of the road. When Henry drove by, they accelerated onto the road behind him.

"Have you had any recent thoughts on the identity of the guy who attacked you yesterday, or who he could be working with?" Henry asked, turning the topic back to the dangerous situation they were dealing with.

From the corner of his eye, Henry could see Rose shaking her head. "No. Believe me, I tried to think of something. But the answer is, no. The whole thing came from completely out of the blue."

"Well, hopefully yesterday will be the last we see of him."

At the courthouse, Henry managed to snag a parking slot close to the entrance. He took a look around, hoping the assailant wasn't desperate enough to take a shot at Rose right here, right now. This was the most vulnerable moment, in Henry's estimation, and the muscles throughout his body were tense.

Henry's cop friends parked in an area that was designated for them. Once they were out of their patrol cars, Henry got Rose out of the truck and the three men surrounded Rose as they escorted her into the courthouse.

In the lobby, Rose pulled out her phone and tapped the screen. "I'm supposed to let the deputy prosecutor, Nate Sloane, know when I've arrived," she told Henry.

Now that Rose had been safely delivered to the court, Kris and Dylan said their goodbyes and headed back out to their patrol cars.

Moments later a side door opened and a well-dressed man with reddish hair, who appeared to be in his early forties, came out to speak to Rose. "I'm glad you've arrived safely. I want to get you on the stand first thing. Come with me."

Rose turned to Henry, her eyes looking a little shiny, and said, "I just want to thank you for everything."

"My pleasure," Henry replied brusquely. She appeared to be on the verge of tears for some reason and he didn't think he could take it if she started crying. She'd been under so much stress over the last twenty-four hours that he wouldn't blame her for breaking down. But if she did, he wasn't sure he could resist wrapping his arms around her, and that wouldn't be good at all. She nodded before turning and disappearing through the double doors into the courtroom alongside the deputy prosecutor.

After a moment's hesitation, Henry decided that since he was already here he might as well hang around and then drive Rose back to get her car, which was still parked at that house she'd inherited. The creeps who'd conspired to kidnap or kill her had been concerned about her testimony, so once that was over she should be fine. But Henry had crossed paths with criminals who committed violent acts purely out of spite or to avenge a bruised ego, so he wanted to make sure yesterday's assailant didn't come after her again just to make himself feel better or to look impressive to his degenerate associates.

Henry would be able to relax as soon as Rose was safely at her home. Then he could turn his full attention back to fixing up his ranch and figuring out the rest of his life.

Rose glanced in her rearview mirror at Henry following behind her in his pickup truck as she drove around the edge of Bear Lake to her condo.

Her time on the witness stand had gone smoothly and she'd been surprised to find Henry waiting for her in the lobby after it concluded. She'd planned on getting a rideshare to take her to pick up her sedan at the inherited house, but Henry had offered to give her a ride there instead and to see her home. He'd pretty much refused to take no for an answer. Admittedly the feeling of being protected by Henry was comforting.

The ride from the courthouse to the loan shark's house was short, so there hadn't been much time to talk about anything other than Rose's relief that she'd given her testimony and the threat to her life was now over. She remained curious about what Kraft might have left for her inside his house, but right now she was still too shaken up over the events of yesterday to want to go inside and look around. She'd go back later, and she'd make sure she had someone with her.

As she rounded a curve in the road that opened up a view of her condominium complex, built atop low rolling hills adjacent to the deep blue water of the lake, Rose organized her thoughts. She wanted to go home and sit with a cup of coffee for a few minutes and collect herself. Then she'd scroll through her work email and maybe make a call to find out the situation awaiting her before she went into the office.

Rose turned onto the entrance road leading into the condo complex and stopped at the security gate. She tapped an app on her phone, and while waiting for the gate to swing open, she took another look at Henry who was still right behind her. He was wearing sunglasses, so she couldn't see his eyes, but his slight head movements let her know he was keeping a close watch on their surroundings.

She could hardly imagine what his life must have been like over the past dozen years to lead him to the point where he was so vigilant all the time. And willing to race into a dangerous situation, like Rose being chased and shot at, without hesitation.

Her gaze lingered a little too long as her attention was drawn to the strong lines of Henry's clean-shaven jaw and his broad shoulders, and he suddenly smiled widely at her. Heat flashed across her cheeks and she turned her attention to the now-open gate in front of her. He'd caught her admiring him and that was annoying.

However, there were moments yesterday afternoon and evening when she'd thought she'd caught him casting an admiring look in her direction, too.

She shook her head, determined to get rid of the feelings that her thoughts were stirring up, and pressed the pedal to drive through the complex entrance.

Rose had gone to Salt Lake City to visit Kendra and the nearby university because she'd wanted to get some forward momentum in a life that had started to feel stagnant. Yes, she had a good job. She was a member of a vibrant church. She had great friends. She traveled. And she spent a lot of time at Cedar Lodge Animal Rescue socializing cats or walking dogs and sometimes even playing with ferrets or brushing horses and mucking out stables if that's what was needed. She kept busy with activities she enjoyed.

And yet she felt as if she should be doing something more. Trying again to earn a college degree seemed like the right move, but the decision to actually do that had not been an easy one.

Over the years she'd been forced to give up on college to help her parents out financially—even though they were perfectly capable of earning the money they needed—and their general irresponsibility had compelled her to hang around and look after them.

Eventually she'd begun to resent that. And then, when she would think about breaking away and living somewhere else for a while even though she loved the beautiful river valley town of Cedar Lodge, she would feel guilty. It had taken some counseling and prayer to get herself ready to go. And then she got the bombshell news that she'd inherited a house.

The thoughts and feelings that followed were overwhelming. But Rose was determined to stick to her plans.

She might enjoy looking at Henry Walsh, but she was not going to get involved with him. The buzz of awareness between them was probably just meaningless flirtation to a former army ranger like him and he was likely used to women throwing themselves at his feet.

Rose was not going to do that.

She drove up to her condo, tapping her phone screen to open her garage door and then closing it behind her after pulling her sedan inside to park. Then she disabled her home alarm and used the interior door to get into her condo. When she opened the front door, Henry was standing there waiting for her. At her invitation, he walked past her into the condo and nerves rippled in her stomach for no particular reason.

"This is a nice place," Henry said, stepping into the foyer. "Mind if I take a quick look around to make sure it's safe?"

"I just turned off the alarm," Rose said. "I'm sure there's no one in here."

Henry raised an eyebrow. "Are you aware it's become fairly common for criminals to use Wi-Fi jammers to disrupt the signals and make home alarm systems virtually useless?"

Rose felt her face blanch. Someone could have crept into her house without her knowing it? She shook her head while gesturing toward the stairs. "Please, look everyplace you think a criminal could be hiding."

Henry nodded, a hint of sympathy in his expression. "I'll make it quick."

He checked the first floor and then jogged upstairs where she could hear him walking around, opening and shutting doors. A few minutes later he came back down. "Everything looks good," he said, after inspecting the lock on her sliding glass door.

"Would you like something to drink?" Rose asked politely when he strode up to her. "I'm going to make coffee, or I have some sun tea in the fridge."

"No, thanks." He grabbed his phone from his pocket. "Call me. Right now."

Rose blinked. "I beg your pardon?"

"I want to make sure we have each other's numbers."

"Oh." She tapped in his number as he rattled it off and then waited for the call to go through before disconnecting.

Henry tapped his screen a few times and then tucked his phone away. "You going to be all right here alone?" he asked, glancing around.

Rose took a deep breath, determined not to let his concern over her safety make her worry when she didn't need to. His former careers had probably left him seeing potential danger around every corner. That was fine for a security professional, but Rose couldn't live that way. She'd be a nervous wreck if she did.

"I'll be fine." She folded her arms across her chest to help settle that electric buzz Henry seemed to be triggering in her body again. "I appreciate everything you've done for me, but I can take care of myself from here."

"Call me if you need me," Henry said. "But since my ranch is relatively far away, call 9-1-1 if you see or hear anything concerning. But after you talk to the dispatcher, call me, too." He cleared his throat. "You've been through a lot and post-traumatic stress is real. I know that from experience. I'm available if you need to talk about that."

He wasn't making it easy for Rose to keep her guard up around him. But she had to. For all the reasons she'd already considered.

She walked him to the door, and after they exchanged goodbyes, she closed it behind him and exhaled a deep breath. Henry Walsh was trouble. Always had been. And she was starting to remember the reason he'd always been trouble for her was that his demeanor would go back and forth between annoyingly teasing to downright gentlemanly in a way that almost made her dizzy. As a teenage girl, she'd known that he could throw off her common sense if she wasn't careful.

It would be best if she stayed away from him, but in the short term that might not be possible. At the very least, they'd likely be brought together by meetings with the police as the cops tried to catch the thug who'd attacked her. She'd just have to guard her heart when she was around Henry.

She started brewing the coffee and then checked her work email, but there wasn't anything in her inbox that was new or appeared important. Her boss must have told her coworkers not to bother her after she'd let him know about the attacks. She wanted to go into the office at least for a short while today since she'd already been gone the couple of weeks on her Utah trip. Later this evening, after she returned home, she would research Gabe Kraft to see if there was anything in his history that she should know about. She'd need to talk to her parents about him, too. At the moment they were aware that she'd come across some trouble after arriving back home in Cedar Lodge but that she was okay. She'd avoided any grim details because she didn't want them to worry.

On the bright side, selling the house she'd just inherited could help pay for her education and that was good. She'd already planned to lease the condo to someone while she was away, but extra money was always welcome.

Of course, she wanted to go through everything in the house before calling a real estate agent to list it. Would the loan shark's family want to buy it? Could they be behind the attacks on her? Were they angry she got the property? She had no way of knowing. And none of those questions addressed the issue of why he'd left it to her in the first place.

Rose poured coffee into a travel mug and took a sip. She might as well leave for the office. Just sitting here at home alone while dwelling on everything that had recently happened no longer held any appeal. Maybe tomorrow she'd check with her friends and see who was willing to go with her to look around at Kraft's house in return for a nice lunch or dinner. She was afraid if she asked Henry to go with her, he would read something into it. She didn't need an armed protector to go with her, anyway, now that her part in the trial was over. She just wanted someone to keep her company because the house felt creepy.

With that idea settled, she grabbed the travel mug, picked up her shoulder bag and walked through the door into her garage, careful to lock the door behind her. She hit the fob to unlock her car, got in and started the engine.

Rose tapped the phone screen to open the garage door and the door started moving.

Bang!

An explosion blew through the space, lifting the back end of her car while shooting heat and glass debris all around her.

Stunned, she gripped her phone while trying to focus her thoughts enough to call 9-1-1. Her heart pounded so hard that her hand shook.

Before she could connect to an emergency dispatcher, a masked intruder appeared beside her sedan door and she screamed. He pounded the safety glass with the barrel of a heavy-duty flashlight until it began to give way.

Lord, help! Rose prayed, as a gloved hand reached inside and locked its grip around her arm.

FOUR

Henry received a call from Kris Volker just as he exited a plumbing supply store in town. Worried that something had happened to Rose, his stomach tightened as he tapped the screen and said, "Yeah, what?"

"There's been a report of an explosion at Rose's condo," Kris said grimly. "I'm almost there." The cop disconnected before giving any further details.

Henry raced to his truck and fired up the engine, determined to get to Rose as fast as he could. He tried to call her and the call went to voicemail. The knot in his stomach cinched tighter and his already-racing heart pounded faster. Rose had given her testimony and her role in the trial was over. Why would someone attack her now?

I should have stayed with her. Guilt and frustration flooded his mind with memories of disastrous times during the course of his career when ops had gone wrong and people had been horrifically injured or killed. Rose was a smart, strong woman with the right to make her own decisions. But having spent her life in Cedar Lodge, she couldn't possibly have witnessed the violence Henry had. She would have a hard time accepting that she could be the target of some deranged criminal through no fault of her own, and that she'd have to change her routine until the attacker was captured and locked up.

Hoping and praying Rose was all right as he drove to her condo, Henry began forming his argument to convince her that she should move back to the ranch and remain there until it was safe for her to leave. Meanwhile, Henry needed to snap out of his own normalcy bias as well. Cedar Lodge was no longer the quiet little low-crime town it used to be. The population had increased dramatically and that meant more crime. It looked as if he'd have to go back to carrying a gun everywhere he went, just like he had as a soldier and international private security contractor. Not exactly the situation he'd hoped for when he'd returned home, but for now at least that was the situation he was dealing with.

Midday traffic was light on the two-lane road following the edge of the lake and Henry made good time. Finally clearing the last turn before Rose's condo complex came into view, he spotted a thin plume of dark smoke reaching toward the sky. Firefighters must be on scene already. But what about Rose?

Henry pressed harder on the gas pedal, finally reaching the condo security gates, which were propped open. At the hilltop at the complex's entrance he came to a halt and quickly surveyed the fire truck and cop cars with flashing lights in the direction of Rose's condo. The roads over there were narrow and Henry didn't want to take his truck in that direction and get in the way of the emergency responders. Additionally, his experience as an incident commander meant he took a broader view of events as they unfolded. Attacks were not always as simple as they first appeared. Getting tunnel vision and assuming the danger would stay in a single confined area was a mistake.

Fear that something terrible had happened to Rose tightened his throat as he tapped his phone to call Kris for an update.

"She's not here," Kris said. "She's not in her car, which is in her garage near the center of the explosion. She's not anywhere in her condo, either."

Please let her be okay, Henry prayed as the breath he'd been holding slowly escaped.

"Neighbors report they saw her being chased," Kris continued. "We're fanning out and searching the complex. K-9 units are on the way."

Rose's condo and the cop cars were to the right of Henry's vantage point. So he'd go left to search for her, where there weren't yet any law enforcement officers looking for her. There was a park in that direction, along with extra storage units for the complex residents and also a private dock on the water's edge. Lots of places for a criminal to take Rose and hide her if that's what was happening.

"I'm on the scene," Henry told Kris. "I'll start searching at the west end of the complex."

"Copy."

Henry drove past the storage units, looking for doors that appeared to have been jimmied open. He rolled down his window. "Rose!" There was no point in being subtle. He wasn't sneaking up on anybody with his truck's rumbling engine. If Rose was still alive—and he would act on that assumption until it was proven wrong—her assailant might have tied her up and left her somewhere with the intention of coming back to get her after law enforcement left the area. The conversation she'd overheard at Kraft's house made it sound as if the criminal's boss preferred that Rose be kidnapped rather than killed. Henry would cling to the shred of hope that that was still the case.

"Rose!" he shouted again, believing she might hear him, and wanting her to know he *would* find her.

He reached a spot that brought him close to the shore of Bear Lake and the private dock with roughly thirty boats moored to it. Movement in the adjacent park caught his attention. Someone was running through the trees toward the water.

Henry got out of his truck and quickly realized he was looking at a dark-haired man with a gun in his hand. The perp approached the dock, moving his head back and forth as he scanned the boats in front of him.

Was Rose on one of those boats?

Bang!

The gunman had spotted Henry and fired at him. Henry ducked behind a tree. He grabbed his phone and placed a brief call to Kris, explaining what was happening.

A siren immediately began wailing near Rose's condo and moving toward the park and the dock.

The gunman glanced toward the sound and then fired several more rounds at Henry, the bullets peeling bark off the tree that was shielding him. Then the creep turned and ran back into the park, disappearing from view.

Finding Rose took priority over capturing that jerk, and Henry raced the length of the nearest pier, looking for her in the open boats while calling her name. When he didn't see her, he retraced his steps, ready to board the vessels with cabins to see if she was hidden inside one of them.

"Rose!" He called out her name again as he reached the first boat with an enclosed deck. He heard her reply, though he couldn't see her or understand what she'd said.

"Rose?" It hadn't sounded as if she was inside the boat closest to him, but she hadn't sounded like she was far away, either.

"Here," she called out.

Henry saw a flash of skin in the water as Rose swam into view. She'd been hiding in the water behind a boat.

Thank You, Lord.

She'd always been smart. As a teenage boy Henry had sometimes been intimidated by her intelligence and he'd reacted by behaving like an immature jerk. But now he was wholeheartedly grateful for it.

He rushed over to haul her out of the water.

"Are you all right?" Henry asked as she stood dripping water onto the pier. He looked her over to see if she had any apparent injuries. "Were you shot or hurt in the explosion at your condo?"

"I'm okay." She began shivering.

Henry didn't have a jacket, so he grabbed some beach towels lying on the seats of a nearby small boat and wrapped them around her shoulders. "I'll return them or pay for them or whatever," he muttered when Rose gave him a wry look. Like the rest of town, she probably assumed at his core he was a thief just like his parents had been. There wasn't anything he could do about that.

The towels didn't appear to be working quickly enough and Henry reached out to wrap his arms around her. When she curled into his embrace, Henry leaned down until his cheek was resting on the top of her head. He wanted to reassure her that she was safe. He also wanted whoever was behind these attacks to pay for what they were doing to her.

A city police car raced up to the end of the dock, followed by a slightly slower-moving EMS vehicle. Kris got out of his cruiser and hurried down the pier toward Henry and Rose. Behind him, paramedic Cole Webb parked the ambulance and jumped out with his medical kit.

"What's the situation?" Kris demanded as he approached.

Rose had stopped shivering and Henry reluctantly released his arms from around her. "Rose is unharmed. The bad guy got away." Henry added the details of the shooter's escape and Kris radioed in the direction the assailant had last been seen headed.

Cole stepped up. "Rosie, how are you doing?"

Behind that low-key persona, Henry knew Cole was a tough former navy medic who was serious about his job.

"My clothes are wet and I'm starving," Rose said. "But otherwise, I'm fine. I don't need medical care."

"Are you sure?" Cole asked cautiously.

She nodded "I am."

"What happened back at your condo?" Kris asked.

"I got in my car to go to work. When I used the app on my phone to open the garage door, there was an explosion." Her voice became shaky and she wiped away the tears that spilled down her cheeks.

Henry took a deep breath to calm his own tumultuous emotions. He wanted to take Rose's hand and offer her reassurance that he would keep her safe, but at the moment that didn't feel appropriate. For all he knew, she might not actually want his personal assurance of anything.

"After the explosion, a man raced into the garage, broke through the side window of my car and grabbed my arm," she continued. "But I twisted free from his grasp and climbed over to the passenger seat where I opened the door and got away. There was a lot of smoke and some plaster and debris still falling in the aftermath of the explosion and that helped me escape because it slowed down the attacker when he tried to come after me.

"He chased me through the complex but I was able to stay ahead of him and throw him off my trail." She sighed deeply, sounding exhausted. "I ended up running over here.

When I saw I was getting close to the docks I figured I'd hide on a boat. But at the last minute I decided to jump into the water and hide *behind* a boat instead. I thought if the shooter found me, I could at least try to swim away."

"That was some quick thinking," Henry said admiringly.

Rose smiled faintly in reply. "I read a lot of books with action and adventure in them." Her attempted smile faded and she crossed her arms tightly over her chest. Tears pooled in her eyes and she shook her head. "I don't understand it. I thought everything would be fine after I gave my testimony. I thought I was out of danger." Her voice broke and tears rolled down her cheeks. "What is happening?" she asked, her gaze fixed on Henry. "What do these people want and why are they still trying to kidnap or kill me?"

"I'd like to know that, too." Henry didn't have an answer. But he was determined to get one and to put an end to these deadly assaults.

"We'll figure it out," Kris said in a grim tone, mirroring Henry's thoughts. "The police department will make this a top priority."

A county sheriff's department cruiser approached the end of the dock and parked behind the ambulance. Deputy Dylan Ruiz got out and walked down the pier toward the others.

"Was this attacker the same loser as yesterday?" Henry asked Rose, his heart aching for her as he watched her wipe away her tears.

She shook her head. "This guy had dark hair."

So it was the guy Henry had seen in the park who'd taken a few shots at him.

"You have any updates for us?" Henry asked Dylan as the deputy approached.

"It was a pipe bomb, not especially strong or sophisticated. A section of the interior of the garage caught fire, but the flames were put out before they could do significant structural damage." Dylan glanced at Rose. "Damage to your car is fairly extensive, though, which I imagine you already know."

Rose shook her head. "I don't understand the point of throwing an explosive into my garage. Why didn't the attacker wait until I backed out and then throw it through a car window if he wanted to kill me?"

"Apparently the goal is still to grab you alive," Henry said. "The bomb was likely intended to make sure your car was too damaged for you to drive away."

"He could have just waited and then shot out my tires," Rose argued.

"Maybe he was afraid you'd be able to get away before he could accomplish that."

An expression of disbelief remained on Rose's face. "Do you think this criminal was waiting for me to come home but didn't do anything at first because you were there?" she demanded of Henry. "And he just happened to have a bomb handy when I tried to leave a little while later?"

"If he's a professional killer or kidnapper he'd have to be ready for anything," Dylan interjected. "And like I said, the device was rudimentary. It wouldn't have taken a criminal mastermind to put it together."

"But it does demonstrate more sophisticated planning than the original attack," Kris commented. He turned to Rose. "And you're sure this was a different guy?"

Rose nodded "The other criminal was skinny and had longish blond hair. This guy was stockier with dark brown hair and eyes."

"So whoever is behind all of this hired the first guy who didn't have much of a plan and probably figured you'd be easy to grab," Henry speculated. "And when that didn't work out, that same behind-the-scenes person hired a thug who was more experienced."

"But why?" Rose asked. "Why is someone still after me?" She chewed on her lower lip for a moment. "And why did Gabe Kraft leave me his house? None of this makes any sense."

"You're right, it doesn't," Kris said. "But we'll work this case until we get to the bottom of it."

"And then we'll get all of the criminals who are involved off the streets," Dylan added.

"Meanwhile, I think you should pack some clothes and stay at the ranch for a while." Henry turned to Rose, bracing for an argument.

"Thank you," she replied. "I'll take you up on that offer."

Henry blinked in surprise at not getting the response he'd anticipated. Back when they were in high school, nearly everything he'd said to her resulted in an argument. Maybe he'd gotten smarter about what he said to her and how he said it. Or perhaps Rose was not as defensive as she'd once been. It was possible they'd both mellowed a little over time.

One thing Henry would not allow to mellow was his determination to protect Rose until the cops captured the criminals who'd assaulted her. If necessary, he'd assist in tracking down those creeps. Because today's attempt proved that the attacks would only increase in danger until the assailants were finally stopped.

Rose looked to Henry's ranch house up ahead as he steered his truck along the driveway. She was grateful to have a place to stay where she might be safe. At the same time she felt disheartened to know her situation had gone from bad to worse since she'd first arrived back in Cedar Lodge roughly thirty-four hours ago after her trip to Utah.

"You're welcome to stay here as long as you need to," Henry said as they rolled along the last section of driveway and up to his home.

Rose cleared her throat. "Thank you." It had been an exhausting afternoon following the attack at her condo. She'd viewed more mug shots at the police station. The new ones were based on her description of the bomb-thrower in her garage, but she hadn't seen the guy in any of them. And then there'd been questions from Kris Volker and even some from Chief Ellis asking about Rose's movements for the last month and who she'd spoken to and what connection she might have had with Gabe Kraft that she'd forgotten to mention or had been too embarrassed to talk about earlier.

Rose hadn't been offended by the questioning because she knew the cops wanted to figure out the motive behind the attacks and put a stop to them. But she hadn't had any new insights to offer. At the moment her spirits were low. She'd really believed that after she gave her testimony in court she would be safe, that the single goal behind the original attack was to prevent her from taking the witness stand. Which in itself seemed so odd, since she'd only witnessed an argument and she hadn't even clearly heard what Kraft and his accused murderer were fighting over.

Now here she was back at Henry's ranch. She had her suitcase and her laptop so she could at least keep up with some of what was happening at work, but beyond that, she had no idea where her life would go next.

"Bad guys make mistakes just like anybody else," Henry said as they got out of his truck and he grabbed Rose's suitcase from the back.

Rose blinked at him. "I'm not sure where you're going with that."

"I'm just saying don't let it get into your head that the assailants who came after you or the person behind the attacks is some kind of mastermind and they'll never get caught. You won't be stuck in limbo hiding out here forever."

Rose was stunned that he could so clearly gauge what she was thinking and feeling. But then she remembered in his former line of work he'd likely experienced situations similar to what she was going through now.

She was grateful that as he spoke he didn't offer her a forced smile backed with manufactured optimism. Instead he looked at her with a quiet confidence that had her thoughts lingering for a moment on the man he'd become over the years they'd been apart. He'd been so flippant and unserious and determined to get a rise out of people when he was a teenager. But now she'd witnessed him being tough and compassionate, focused and brave.

She was curious to know what had changed him. And given that his parents were drug dealers who'd been arrested for breaking and entering and petty theft several times over the years—everybody at school knew about it—how had he turned out so different from them?

"What kept you from following the same path as your parents?" Rose asked as they walked in the front door of the house.

His expression suddenly shuttered. That was not the reaction she had expected. What was wrong? Her question had obviously been intended as a compliment.

"You think I might have inherited some criminal tendencies from my mom and dad?" Henry asked in a breezy tone that didn't at all match the defensive way he now looked.

"Do you think growing up around them and their sleazy friends must have rubbed off on me?"

Rose shook her head. "No." She didn't know what to say to steer the conversation back in the direction she wanted it to go. "I just think any kid would be influenced by the situation they grew up in."

"I'm sure you're right," he said, cutting her off before she could finish her thought and tell him she admired people who worked to overcome negative influences on their lives.

He strode toward the bedroom where she'd stayed before and she followed him. He placed her suitcase beside the bed and she wanted to apologize but the tension she now felt coming from him made her think this might not be the best time.

"Let me know if you need anything," he said, his tone genuinely polite, though more aloof than it had been a short while ago. "I imagine you want to rest. You've been through a lot, I'm sorry for that, and you must be exhausted. I need to get a little work done while it's still light outside."

"Of course."

He walked out of the room and Rose felt a pang of loss. She must have offended him. Because he was wild Henry Walsh, it hadn't even occurred to her that he might have a few tender spots in his life that she should tread carefully around. She shook her head. She should have known better.

Resting in her room by herself didn't have much appeal. She wanted a glass of cool water to ease the scratchy feeling that remained in her throat after inhaling smoke following the garage explosion, so she went into the kitchen where she ran into Bennie. Through the kitchen window she could see Vivien outside, working to trim back the riotous growth of blackberry vines.

"Can I help with dinner?" Rose asked, smelling something delicious cooking while she got her glass of water.

Bennie grinned. "I've got my world famous slow-cooker chile relleno casserole going." He lifted the lid on a pot on the counter and the wonderful spicy scent made Rose's stomach rumble. "I'll start some Mexican rice a little later, but I don't need any help. Appreciate the offer, though."

"Sure." Rose drank her glass of water, refilled it, then stepped outside.

Henry walked out of a nearby shed carrying a toolbox and headed toward a section of fence that Rose had seen him working on yesterday. She finished her water and set the glass on the porch railing near Melvin the cat, then walked over to Henry, determined to get things right between them again.

He'd already started hammering a nail when she walked up, but as she drew close, he stopped.

"When my mom and dad were young, they had a dream of escaping the corporate lifestyle of their parents," she said, wanting him to know that she didn't come from a perfect family, either. "They moved here to Montana with the goal of living a kind of idealized, unstructured life. A Bohemian lifestyle, you might call it. I was born and they structured their lives a little more, but not much. Everything was uncertain when I was growing up."

Henry shifted his weight, watching her closely but not saying anything.

Rose took a deep breath. "We stayed in Cedar Lodge, but within town we moved a lot. Especially when I was little. My parents weren't serious about holding down jobs. Money was scarce at times. They got into problems with debt, repeatedly impulse-buying things they didn't need and couldn't afford. A compulsion with miserable results that continued until just a couple of years ago."

Henry looked at her, and the lines of tension that had appeared in response to her earlier comment about *his* family had eased. "That must have been rough."

"As far as I can tell, their behavior is what led me to being a bit of a control freak who worries about details and gets concerned when things don't appear to be well-organized."

She paused but Henry didn't say anything, so she took another breath and continued. "I mentioned the situation with you and your parents because I know how much my parents impacted me, and even when you love them—and I do love my mom and dad, underneath it all they really are good and loving people—it's hard to choose to live differently from them and then act on that." She shrugged. "That's all I was saying."

She watched him for a response.

He pressed his lips together and then lifted an eyebrow. "A *bit* of a control freak? You think you were just *a bit* of a control freak in high school?" He scoffed and Rose laughed, and it felt as if the tension between them fell away.

"No hard feelings," he said. "I'll keep you safe until we can get your situation figured out and the criminals behind it locked up," Henry said in a reassuring tone that gave Rose a tickling sensation in the pit of her stomach. She tried to quell it because she didn't want to let herself be attracted to Henry only to end up getting her heart broken. Unfortunately there didn't seem to be much she could do about it. Despite her best intentions, that thrilling sensation was still there.

"The police are going after the attackers and I appreciate that," she said, forcing her attention away from her emotions. "While they're doing that, I need to figure out what's behind Gabe Kraft leaving me that house. Why did he do it? The attacks and my inheritance of that place have got to be connected. I just don't know how."

"We'll do our best to figure it out," Henry said. "Both of us."

"Thank you." His generous offer to help was deeply appreciated. Rose just hoped she could stay alive long enough to get this aggravating mystery figured out. She also hoped she wouldn't put Henry in a position where he would get injured or killed investigating all of this alongside her.

FIVE

"All right, that's done," Rose said to Henry early the following morning. She pocketed her phone and sat down in a chair on the wooden deck behind the ranch house, taking in the gorgeous view of the thick forest and nearby mountain range.

"I told Mr. Holmes that I needed to take another week off, but that I'd come into the office if he really wanted me to," Rose continued after picking up her mug of coffee from an overturned wooden crate that served as a table. Emmett Holmes was a kind older gentleman who'd hired Rose eight years ago and then offered her every opportunity to work her way up to becoming the general manager of his insurance sales office.

"I feel guilty taking off more time after having just had a two-week vacation in Utah," she added. "But I'd feel even worse if Mr. Holmes or any of my coworkers were injured if I got attacked while I was at work." Her gaze shifted to Henry. "I worry that something bad could happen here, too, and that you or Bennie or Vivien would get hurt."

"Don't worry about us," Henry responded. The determined expression in his eyes reminded her that he had experience protecting people and dealing with dangerous situations.

Rose broke her gaze away from Henry's when Bennie stepped outside to join them with his own steaming cup of coffee in hand and the energetic long-haired Chihuahua, Buster, hot on his heels. Bennie dropped into a chair and Buster immediately hopped up into his lap.

"So what's the plan for today, Boss?" Bennie asked Henry.

Rose's shoulders dropped and she shook her head slightly. *Of course* they had tasks to accomplish around the ranch, and here she was throwing a dangerous wrench into things. "I know chores and things need to get done," she said, her face warming in embarrassment, "so let's make your to-do list the priority and we can plan whatever I need to do around that."

"It's fine," Henry said dismissively. "Your safety is paramount. The repairs we're doing aren't on a tight schedule. We still have a couple of months before we need to finish the outside projects and prep the ranch for winter."

Did he really not have a schedule for everything he hoped to accomplish? The interior of the house was in good shape, but Rose knew they planned to install a new sink and vanity in the hall bathroom and after that they intended to put new flooring down. She'd also overheard them talking about the fencing around the meadow in front of the house and repairs to a couple of gates in the corral, and how did Henry expect to get all of that taken care of before snow started to fall?

Not Rose's concern, and yet it bugged her. Did Henry have a lackadaisical streak that Rose hadn't seen yet? Was he like her parents who were great on making plans and terrible on following through? Of course the world needed all types of people and everyone didn't need to be a focused planner such as herself, but she could never build a life with a man who just took everything as it came with minimal forethought. Not that she and Henry had a relationship that included the possibility of a future together. Still, her thoughts went in that direction.

"I can practically see your brain going into overdrive," Henry commented to Rose. "I know it's easy to say and sometimes hard to do, but try not to worry. We'll get you squared away and the ranch taken care of before winter hits and everything will be fine."

Would everything be fine? She took a deep breath and blew it out. *Lord, I know my life is in Your hands and I trust You.* She needed to send up that prayer and give herself that reminder more often.

"How about this," she began, because they *did* need a plan. "How about we go take a look at the house Gabe Kraft left me right now? If we don't find anything notable, which seems likely, though I hate to admit it, we'll come back here and you'll have the rest of the day to do what you need to."

"Why don't you think you'll find anything helpful?" Bennie asked.

"Because Kraft's family and their lawyer indulged in some shady ethics to drag things out for as long as possible before letting me know I'd inherited the house. The man died nearly a year ago and I just found out about my inheritance. His family has obviously rifled through the property and taken what they wanted—the brief look around the house that I've already had makes that evident—so I doubt they've allowed anything significant to be left behind. Including any kind of physical clue or letter if he had indeed wanted to communicate with me and let me know why he gave me his house." Thinking about it last night, she'd realized it was best not to get her hopes up.

Henry got to his feet. "Let's go right now."

Rose stood and followed him into the house, with Bennie trailing behind.

"We're heading out," Henry called to Viv, who was in the kitchen with bowls full of fresh blackberries set along the counter.

"Okay," she called out as her husband walked toward her and Henry and Rose continued out through the front door. Melvin the cat was in his usual spot on the porch railing and Rose gave his head a scratch as she walked by.

When they reached the pickup truck, Henry pulled a pistol from beneath his T-shirt at the small of his back and placed the weapon inside the truck's center console. Rose's breath caught at the sight of the weapon. It wasn't as if she'd forgotten she was in danger, but the stark reminder was sobering.

After starting up the vehicle and heading down the long driveway, Henry called Kris on the truck's hands-free device.

"What do you want?" the cop asked his friend after he picked up the call.

"Just checking to see if you have an update regarding the attacks on Rose."

"If I had anything to tell you, I would have told you by now. You know that."

"Fair enough. She and I are heading over to Gabe Kraft's old house to have a look around."

"Copy. I'll try to patrol in that area so I'm available for backup if there's more trouble. Can't promise anything, though. I keep getting tied up with ridiculous traffic stops. How hard is it to respect basic safety rules when you're driving so people don't get killed?"

"Hey, Kris, you know what?" Henry asked.

"What?"

"You're turning into a cranky old man."

"Whatever," Kris said before disconnecting.

Henry laughed and the low rumble sent a wave of warmth through Rose.

"It's amazing you're still friends with Kris and Dylan and Cole after all the time you've spent apart."

Henry shrugged. "There are some people you just have a connection with. Even though at times it defies logic."

The were getting closer to the highway and his demeanor changed as he sat up straighter and focused more intently on their surroundings.

A ripple of nerves moved through Rose and she began looking around more carefully for possible attackers, too.

At least this time when arriving at the property she'd inherited she would be aware of the potential for danger. She glanced at the console where the gun was stored. And Henry would be armed. Her stomach twisted anxiously, nevertheless. Much as she liked to believe that being prepared and having a plan guaranteed that everything would go well, she could admit to herself that it wasn't always the case.

She looked at Henry as they made the turn onto the highway, her gaze lingering on his clenched jaw. He was concerned about what might happen while they were at the Kraft house, too. She'd put him in harm's way by asking for his help. And yeah, he could handle himself in a dangerous situation and look out for her—he'd proven that. Still, knowing that about him didn't make her feel any less nervous.

Henry opened the door of Gabe Kraft's former house and flicked the nearby wall switch. A lamp in the corner of the front room began to glow.

"Good, the electricity has been connected," Rose murmured behind him.

"We need to order you one of those inexpensive security camera systems for this place ASAP," Henry said before doing a quick sweep of the rooms and closets in the house with Rose right behind him. The air inside was stale and there wasn't the *feel* of someone having recently been in there ahead of them. There weren't any fresh footprints or tire tracks outside the house, either, but Henry wasn't taking anything for granted. Especially when it came to keeping Rose safe.

"Looks good," he said, tucking away his gun at the small of his back as they returned to the front room.

"This place needs some fresh air." Rose walked into the kitchen to open the small window above the sink.

"Maybe open it just a crack and keep the curtains closed so no one can see you and potentially take a shot at you." Henry opened another window a little bit.

"What's next?" he asked Rose.

She glanced around at the desk and file cabinets and the few pieces of living room furniture and then shifted her gaze toward the other end of the house. "There isn't much in the bedrooms or the bathroom. Let's look in them first for anything interesting, that should go quickly, and then work our way back to the kitchen and out here to the office area."

"Sounds good. What are we looking for?"

"I don't know, that's the problem." She tucked her sable hair behind her ears. "I don't even know for sure that Kraft left anything here for me to find. I'm just guessing that he might have. And even if he did, his family members could have already taken it. They certainly weren't shy about helping themselves to anything they wanted." She gestured toward the pass-through to the kitchen where the stove and refrigerator were missing and the cabinet doors hung open with the shelves empty, giving the place a ransacked look.

Henry took a step toward the desk, noting the absence of a computer, tablet or printer. "Looks like any item of monetary value has been taken, but all these physical files are left behind. Seems like they might be worth something to his family if they're in the loan-sharking business, too. What do you know about his family?"

Rose shrugged. "Not much. According to the lawyer who contacted me on their behalf, they don't live in Cedar Lodge. I assume they were hoping to sell the property and keep the cash but my inheritance got in their way."

She'd already starting walking toward the back bedroom and Henry followed her.

Rose opened a closet door and pulled out a couple of boxes, dumping the contents on the floor and then rifling through them. "Just winter clothes," she said, "and most of them look old and well-worn." Hangers clanked as she took a look at the few items still dangling from the rod.

Henry turned and lifted a box spring and mattress from the floor—there was no bed frame or headboard—and he searched the underside of the box spring before turning the mattress over to check it more closely.

"What are you doing?" Rose asked, coming up behind him.

"Looking for a slit in the mattress or a handsewn seam or a strange lump that would suggest something was hidden inside."

"You really are thorough," she noted.

After finding nothing out of the ordinary, Henry dropped the mattress. Rose was still nearby, and when he looked at her, he noticed several strands of hair matted to the side of her forehead. The air might be circulating near the open windows in the front of the house, but back here it was still stuffy. Henry found himself wanting to reach out and wipe aside the dampened hair for her, but it might not be a welcomed gesture and he didn't blame her. He was here to help and protect her, not to become overly familiar.

In fact, letting himself become distracted by her was a mistake. It was a challenge he hadn't been required to deal with recently. Of course Henry had worked around attractive women, but none of them had tugged at his focus and concentration the way Rose did when she was nearby.

"I've tossed a lot of rooms over the years looking for clues or evidence," he said in reply to her comment. "People who've been held captive and then moved to a new location sometimes leave a hidden note behind."

"Oh," Rose said, wide-eyed.

Maybe she'd never thought about the ugly realities of Henry's career. *Former career,* he reminded himself.

They moved to the second bedroom and went through the same process in their search. This time Rose took longer, since there were several boxes stacked in the closet and she wanted to look through them herself. Henry stood by while she did that. None of the stuff appeared interesting. Just more old clothes and blankets and some aged sports equipment.

They moved on to the bathroom and the kitchen, and there was nothing there that seemed important, either.

"Well, it's obvious now we should have started here," Rose said as they walked back to the combination living room and office in the front room of the house.

"It's only obvious now because we looked in the other places first," Henry said. He turned over the sofa to look beneath it, and finding nothing hidden there, he checked the cushions and then moved on to searching an end table with an attached cabinet. While he worked, he was vaguely aware of the sounds of Rose opening and closing desk drawers and then file cabinet drawers.

He finally glanced over to see that she had several stacks of file folders and papers along with photos lined up atop the desk. Henry supposed he could have come up with a method for organizing the items if he'd had to, but he wouldn't have done it nearly as efficiently as Rose.

After manhandling a recliner chair, searching it and then setting it back in place, Henry glanced at Rose again and was surprised to see her seated at the desk chair with one hand over her mouth while she stared at something inside an open file folder.

"What is it?" he asked, hustling over in her direction. "What have you found?"

"My parents," she said, sounding as if she were about to cry. "After all we went through, after all the promises to never do it again, they took out a second loan from Gabe Kraft after we paid off the first one."

"Oh, no." Henry's heart sank in sympathy with Rose.

"Oh, yes. It looks like they did it about three months before Kraft was murdered."

"So they didn't have to pay the loan back," Henry said, wincing as he realized how callous he sounded.

"My grandparents on both sides had money," Rose said, her attention still focused on the paper she was staring at. "But my mom and dad thought they wanted a less materialistic lifestyle. Until they got older and started really missing the *stuff*. Cars, nice clothes, whatever. And they began spending beyond their means and they just couldn't stop."

"I don't know if it's something similar or not, but I finally figured out that *my* parents had an emptiness inside them that they tried to quiet with drugs or fill with stuff they could buy thanks to the money they made stealing things or drug dealing," Henry said.

Rose turned to him, tears glinting in her eyes. Henry felt a sharp pain in his heart mirroring the emotions he imagined she felt right now.

"I think my mom and dad were somewhat the same as yours," Rose said. "After I came to faith and experienced peace in my heart, I could see how much they were lacking peace and a sense of fulfillment. I convinced them to go to church with me a few times, but it wasn't something they were really interested in and I have to respect their right to make their own way through life."

Henry moved one of the file stacks so he could sit on the edge of the desk.

Rose took a deep breath and blew it out, then wiped away her tears.

"How did you find your parents' file?" Henry asked.

Rose gestured toward a nearby file cabinet drawer that was still partially open. "I looked in here. This drawer is easiest to reach while still seated in this chair," she said. "I figured it would have the most recent files that Kraft referenced most often."

She turned toward the stacks of folders on the desk. "It'll take a while to go through all of these."

Henry got to his feet. "Okay, while you work on that I'll go through all the drawers again just to make sure there isn't a hidden key or flash drive or anything tucked away in there."

"You know what I think?" Rose asked.

Henry gave her his full attention. "What do you think?"

"I think it's possible Gabe Kraft knew his life was in danger—it probably always was to some degree given the way he chose to live—and he kept something here that could point to the most likely killer if he did indeed end up murdered."

Henry thought for a moment. "And Kraft had seen how meticulous you are. So maybe he gambled on the chance that if you inherited his house, you'd go through the files and eventually figure out what had transpired if something nefarious did in fact happen to him."

"I don't suppose he could count on his relatives to do anything like that."

Henry nodded. "It could turn out that the guy who's being charged with Kraft's murder, Lance Preston, really is the culprit. But, then again, maybe he isn't. Last night I read some online articles about the murder case to get caught up. Lance claims that he's being framed."

"He's said that from the start."

Henry began a search of the file cabinet, upending the drawers and pulling the cabinet away from the wall to look behind it, but he didn't find anything. When he finished and turned to Rose, she was again staring at a piece of paper in a file folder.

"Thomas Conway and Dora Ross," Rose read aloud as Henry walked to her. "I know these people. And the dates on these papers are within weeks of Kraft's murder."

"They took out loans from him, too?"

Rose slowly shook her head. "I don't know. My parents' paperwork is a pretty straightforward balance sheet indicating money loaned to them and their subsequent payments back to Kraft. There are a bunch of files that look like that. But these two are different. They have a mixture of words and numbers written on them. Like a code." She rubbed her forehead. "I can't get anywhere with this. There's no way to figure it out."

Footsteps near the front of the house caught Henry's attention before he could say anything to encourage her.

"Hide under the desk," he told Rose, having already drawn the pistol he'd tucked beneath his waistband. His attention was focused on the front door and tension tightened his muscles. He could hear a single individual climbing up the steps, but there could be an additional accomplice staged nearby.

"Get ready to call 9-1-1," Henry said quietly. He stepped toward a window intending to move the curtain aside and look out, but before he could do that someone pounded on the door.

Assailants didn't typically knock before entering. But Henry couldn't help thinking of Rose's story regarding Gabe Kraft first presenting himself as a nice guy. What easier way could there be for an assailant to enter a house than to start out with a straightforward knock on the door?

Henry moved the curtain and got a partial view of a man out there. That didn't tell him much. Standing behind the door so he could use it as a barrier if he needed to, Henry pulled it open.

SIX

"I guess you're my new neighbor?" Rose heard an unfamiliar voice say from the front porch.

"You live nearby?" Henry asked suspiciously.

Rose moved to see the visitor. They guy looked maybe ten years older than Rose and Henry, with brown hair that was gelled and combed straight back.

The man spotted Rose and lifted his hand in a slight wave. "Hi. My name's Curtis Tucker." Curtis turned his attention back to Henry, who continued to block the doorway. "I live on the next street over." He hooked a thumb toward the back of the house. "I saw the truck parked out here and figured it might be a good time to meet my new neighbor." He extended a blue metal tin filled with butter cookies. "A small welcome gift," he said, with a self-conscious shrug.

Rose reached around Henry to take it. "Thank you. I'm Rose Balfour and this is Henry Walsh. Please, come in."

She could tell Henry wasn't thrilled with her invitation, but the man seemed harmless and Rose wanted to be on friendly terms with her new neighbor. Maybe he'd be able to give them some helpful information about Gabe Kraft.

Henry stepped aside, with obvious reluctance, to let Curtis come inside.

"I'd offer you something to drink," Rose said after setting down the cookie tin, "but as you can see, there's no fridge in the kitchen and not even a coffee maker."

"I'm fine," Curtis said. "And I don't want to get in your way. I just came over to introduce myself and encourage you to come over and get me if you need anything. Moving is hard." He heaved out a sigh while glancing around. "Cleaning the place out will be a lot of work. Getting settled always takes longer than you think."

"I'm not moving in," Rose told him.

"Are you selling the place?" Curtis asked, looking interested.

"Sell it or lease it, I suppose." Rose figured she'd make that decision later.

"So, did you know your neighbor was a loan shark who employed violent means when necessary to procure his payments?" Henry asked Curtis.

Rose held back a sigh. She was trying to make friends with her neighbor and Henry was on the verge of antagonizing the guy.

"I kind of did *and* didn't know what Gabe was up to," Curtis said after a long hesitation. "I only learned the details after he was murdered and the information showed up in the news."

"How can you know and not know?" Rose asked. She gestured toward the sofa and chairs and the three of them sat down.

"Gabe bought the place about six years ago," Curtis said after he was seated. "And that winter, we had the ice storm. You remember that?"

Rose nodded.

"A couple of my trees fell over here onto Gabe's property. They damaged a section of the chain-link fence and pretty much demolished his gardening shed. I came over to talk to him about it and he was cool. The only thing he wanted was for me to get the trees off his property and fix the fence. Said not to worry about the shed."

"And you became friends?" Rose asked.

Curtis shrugged. Then he chewed nervously on his lower lip. "People came and went at odd hours. Sometimes there were loud parties. A few times I could hear fights. People yelling, maybe someone getting smacked around, that kind of thing." Curtis's gaze had dropped to his feet but now he lifted it to look Rose straight in the eye. "If I had heard gunshots or anything like that, I would have called the police."

"But you didn't call about the other stuff," Henry said.

"I got the idea he was a criminal and I was afraid to stir up trouble. Besides, he'd come over or send somebody over to apologize when anything disruptive happened. It sort of felt like a threat. But then he also sent over a nice basket at Christmas every year. It was an odd situation."

"But you knew he was a criminal?" Henry pressed.

"I knew he was somebody that I wanted to stay on good terms with." Curtis gestured toward the file cabinet. "I was over here for some reason, I can't remember what, and I told him I had a sixteen-year-old nephew who could digitize some of those old files if he wanted to do that. Gabe had computers and Wi-Fi here, but he said that nothing stored digitally on an internet-connected device was completely secure. Said he knew the basics of online security but wasn't an expert so he didn't want to take any chances."

Rose nodded. That explained why Gabe Kraft had kept his crime-related notes on paper in an old-school file cabinet. In a way it was surprising, but for a criminal it also made sense.

"He told me he researched property titles for a living," Curtis said. "I took him at face value because I didn't want any trouble. It was only when his murder made the news that I learned about his loan-sharking business."

"Have you seen any unusual activity over here since Kraft died?" Henry asked.

"Not really. His cousin and I think a brother-in-law showed up with a trailer and took some of the furniture and appliances from the house shortly after Gabe died, but that's about it." Curtis looked around, and after a short lull in the conversation, he got to his feet. "Well, it's been nice to meet you."

"Thank you for the cookies," Rose said, walking him to the door.

"If you decide to sell this place, please let me know. I'd be interested in buying it to fix it up and make it a rental."

Rose closed the door behind him. She turned to Henry, who'd lifted the edge of the curtain to watch Curtis walk away. "What do you think?"

"I think this is not the time to trust anybody you don't already know." He dropped the curtain and turned to her. "Not everyone who is a threat will show up looking like one."

"I'll remember that," Rose said before going back to her stacks of file folders.

"If you want, we could pack up all the files and haul them back to the ranch where you could take your time going through all of them," Henry offered an hour later.

"I'm ready to go. I've set aside the things I want to look at more closely." She tapped her finger on a piece of paper. "I found the balance sheet for Lance Preston confirming that he hadn't been making payments and was accruing interest very quickly. Allegedly, that's the reason he murdered Kraft. Beyond the other papers I already mentioned, nothing else here really jumps out at me." She rubbed her eyes. "A lot of the papers in these files are fairly old and most of them are just simple ledgers showing payments received. The more recent ones have that alphanumeric code I mentioned that I obviously don't understand, and I haven't come across any other names that I recognize."

"So we're done here for now?" Henry hoped Curtis was simply the friendly neighbor he appeared to be, but it was possible that he wasn't. Henry's gut instinct nudged him to get Rose out of the house before anybody else showed up.

"Yeah, we might as well go back to the ranch," Rose said slowly, sounding a little distracted. "I'm just wondering what we should do about the files I've pulled aside that I think are significant."

"What do you mean?"

She rubbed her chin and then let her hand drop. "I feel like we should let law enforcement or somebody in the justice system know that these files are here. I'm sure the cops came to the house after Kraft was murdered, but maybe no one looked carefully through the files. And maybe there's some information in them that could help with open criminal cases. Maybe there's evidence pointing to somebody else who borrowed money and couldn't pay and wanted Gabe Kraft dead."

"Considering that Kraft took advantage of his victims' desperation, I imagine there are a lot of people who want him dead. Of course Lance Preston is going to claim he's not guilty, but don't you think the case looks pretty clear-cut?"

"Preston is an admitted alcoholic who was found passed out holding the gun that killed Kraft. That's so blatant that it kind of looks like he could have been framed, don't you think?"

Henry let go a laugh and dragged his hand through his hair. "You want to add an investigation into the Gabe Kraft murder case onto your plate alongside trying to figure out why the loan shark left you a house and, oh, yeah, trying to stay alive while people try to kill you?" Frustration with Rose tightened his jaw muscles.

Admittedly, he admired that she cared about the truth and she had the intellectual aptitude to research and look into details. But at the same time he could see how she was inclined to put too much on her shoulders. Maybe it came from the situation with her parents where she'd been pretty much looking after them while she was still a kid herself. It was likely a compulsive behavior, but he wanted to help her stop it so that her life would be easier.

"No, I don't want to look into the murder," Rose said, dropping her shoulders. "I just feel I should tell somebody about all of this."

Henry shook his head and took a few steps away while Rose pondered what she wanted to do. He could feel himself getting way too involved in her personal life and caring about her way too much. A protector by nature, he didn't have a problem with wanting to keep her safe. But the craving to know her better and offer her his personal opinion was dangerous territory and he was smart enough to realize when it was time to retreat.

She had plans to go away to college. He had no idea what he was going to do beyond fixing up the ranch and possibly arranging for Bennie and Viv to live there until they could afford to buy it. Last night he'd found himself thinking about how they looked so happy and at home there. Maybe his original plan for a quick sale of the property wasn't the best idea. Perhaps he should just let them stay and look after the place for a while.

Henry already knew he didn't want to settle back in the small—but growing—town where too many people knew about the rough conditions he'd grown up under and weren't quite sure how trustworthy he really was. Maybe Rose still kept some of her old impressions of him from years ago in the back of her mind. Maybe more recently after seeing him, she'd let some of her bad opinions of Henry go. But there was no way he was going to put himself in a romantic situation—or any kind of situation—where he continually felt compelled to prove himself. He'd had enough of that.

"Let's go by the deputy prosecutor's office on the way back to the ranch and I'll drop off these papers," Rose finally said. "I know he's likely at the trial since it's still ongoing, but I'll leave a note with his administrative assistant telling him there's potentially more information here that he'd be interested in. If he doesn't care about it, I guess I'll go ahead and throw everything out when I clean the house."

"After you've looked at every single item," Henry muttered.

"Possibly," Rose replied.

Maybe Rose actually had figured out why Kraft had left her the house. That he wanted her to solve his murder. But that didn't address the question of why assailants were coming after her. And if they were concerned about the files—or the information contained in them—why hadn't they broken in and taken them while the house was sitting empty over the last several months?

Rose had her phone out and was taking pictures of the files she intended to turn over to the deputy prosecutor. "I need to have my own copies because I want to talk to my parents about this. I want them to see proof that I know they took out another loan." She returned Henry's gaze when he looked at her. "I also want to talk to Dora Ross and Thomas Conway and see if they can tell me what this code written beside their names means."

"Okay."

After she was finished with her photos, Henry opened the door and made sure it was safe before they stepped outside. At this point Rose might be in more danger if she *didn't* continue her investigation. Following the trail of information in the files Kraft left behind might be the only way—or at least the fastest way—to stop the attacks on her if it revealed who was behind them.

Acknowledging that, however, didn't stop Henry from wanting to hide her at the ranch while he conducted the investigation on her behalf. Not a realistic possibility since he didn't personally know anyone mentioned in the files, and they likely wouldn't open up to him the way they would to Rose. But the desire to keep her safely hidden was there, nevertheless.

"Judge Markham decided to put the trial on hold for a couple of days after the third attack on you," Cedar Lodge Deputy Prosecutor Nate Sloane said to Rose as he gestured for her and Henry to take a seat in front of his desk. "Some of the jurors are scared."

Rose had been surprised to find Sloane at his office when she and Henry stopped by to drop off the file folder she'd found at the house along with a note explaining why she'd left it for him.

"The trial is scheduled to resume at the beginning of next week," he continued. "We're hoping the jurors who were concerned will feel safe enough to continue with the trial by then."

"Hopefully there won't be any more attacks," Rose said, though her tone didn't convey much confidence. She didn't know the reason for the assaults so she couldn't know what might make them stop. There had been no demands made of her, no verbal or written threats to indicate why she'd been targeted other than the original reference to her trial testimony. The attack after she'd taken the witness stand and then returned home made no sense at all.

"You said something when you arrived about having papers for me to look at?" Sloane prompted.

Rose took the folder she'd been holding and leaned forward to hand it to him. "There's a file cabinet full of papers inside the house I inherited from Gabe Kraft. This particular folder contains notes from some of his criminal business transactions shortly before he was murdered. There's information about the loans he gave people, including my parents." Her face heated with embarrassment, but she refused to look away. "And there are other transactions I can't figure out with some kind of code referencing them."

Sloane opened the folder and briefly flipped through the papers before turning his gaze back to Rose. "Kraft is deceased, obviously, so I don't know why you brought this to me." He set the folder on his desk. "I'm certainly not going to prosecute anyone who was a victim of his loan-sharking operation."

"I just felt like this information might be important," Rose replied, second-guessing her impulse to show the paperwork to someone of authority in the justice system.

"We already know Lance Preston murdered Gabe Kraft," Sloane said dismissively. "We've got the weapon, we have Preston's fingerprints on that weapon, we have motive and you personally witnessed him arguing with Kraft the day before the murder. There's no potential for finding some other viable suspect in those files if that's what you're thinking."

"If that's true, then why do these thugs keep coming after Rose?" Henry asked.

The deputy prosecutor shrugged. "I suppose it's possible we'd find something in these files that would give us insight into that, but it strikes me as unlikely."

"So the files are not something you're interested in?" Rose asked.

Sloane shook his head and handed the folder back to Rose.

"Maybe we should take it to the police department and see if they're interested in looking at these files or any of the others," Henry said to her.

"Chief Ellis has to accomplish a lot on a limited budget, like so many of us these days," Sloane said. "Lots of people moving in puts a greater demand on public services, but the tax revenue to fund those services and hire additional employees hasn't shown up yet. Not in large enough numbers." The deputy prosecutor leaned back in his chair. "Maybe if the files were in digital form it would be worth searching through them for potential connections to other crimes in town, including the attacks on you, but that idea really is a long shot. However, I'd encourage you to go ahead and talk to Chief Ellis if you want to and see what he says."

Discouragement pressed heavily on Rose's shoulders. The information in the files was probably too random to be of much use, and she really had no idea what those mysterious codes meant.

And yet, those two names she recognized in that file, Dora Ross and Thomas Conway, stuck in her mind. Maybe she should let go of all the other paperwork and instead just focus on talking to those two people. Maybe they could tell her what that code on their files meant, and uncovering that might lead her toward the information Gabe Kraft had wanted her to find. Maybe after she spoke with Dora and Thomas, she'd have some idea of who wanted her kidnapped or dead, and why.

Sloane's phone rang and he glanced at it. "I'll need to take this."

"Of course." Rose got to her feet, and Henry did as well. "I appreciate you taking the time to meet with us."

"Of course." Sloane reached for his phone while Rose and Henry headed for the door.

Outside the city government building, Henry wrapped his arm around Rose and pulled her close in a side hug as they walked toward his truck. "Believe it or not, following a potential information trail and learning that it's a dead end is actually forward progress," he said.

Rose scoffed, but having his arm around her felt good so she leaned into him despite disbelieving what he'd said. The added warmth and the feel of his muscles gave her a sense of strength and security she needed right now. After walking for a few moments like that, she felt her spirts lift. "I suppose it isn't reasonable to think every avenue you go down will offer a payoff," she said.

Henry nodded. "If you aren't making mistakes, you likely aren't making progress, either."

They got into his truck and he drove out of town. It was near midday and there wasn't much traffic on the highway. They drove a few miles while Rose tapped the names of Dora Ross and Thomas Conway into her phone to see what kind of information she could find. She'd been vaguely aware of Henry keeping an eye on their surroundings as they drove, but now she could see from the corner of her eye that he was checking his rearview mirror with increasing regularity and intensity.

"What is it?" she asked, putting away her phone.

"I'm not sure," he said, his voice tense, "but I think we're being followed."

They drove past the turn they normally took to get back to the ranch.

"I don't want to make it obvious where you're staying," Henry said, anticipating her question.

They drove farther along the highway. Looking into her side mirror Rose could see a dark blue heavy-duty SUV behind them. "Is it the SUV you're worried about or one of the cars farther back?" she asked.

"The SUV."

A road sign indicated an intersection ahead.

"I'm going to turn off the highway and see what the SUV does," Henry said.

"Okay."

He took his foot off the accelerator, but didn't hit the brake to turn onto the unpaved county road until the last minute. Rose grabbed the door handle to steady herself. Henry quickly made a U-turn so the truck faced the highway.

The SUV drove by.

But then its taillights flared as the driver braked and made his own U-turn. Seconds later, the SUV was barreling back in their direction.

"Hang on!" Henry hit the gas and drove onto the highway, heading back toward downtown Cedar Lodge.

SEVEN

"I'm calling the cops!" Rose struggled to pull her phone from her pocket while remaining upright in her seat as Henry sped up along a curving section of highway.

The call connected, not always a certainty on the edges of a town tucked between tall mountain peaks. "9-1-1, what's your emergency?"

"We're being chased on the highway!"

Bang!

A bullet struck the back window of the truck and Rose felt her gut knot with fear.

"Get down!" Henry yelled.

"Ma'am, what was that sound?" the dispatcher asked with calm intensity.

"We're being shot at," Rose hollered over the phone, sliding down in her seat and trying to be heard above the loud rumbling of the truck's engine. She called out their general location and the direction they were heading.

"Give them a physical description of my truck and the SUV chasing us," Henry said.

His intensely focused yet calm demeanor mirrored that of the emergency dispatcher, and for a split second Rose's thoughts flickered toward what he must have experienced in his life for him to behave as if this situation were relatively normal.

Rose described the vehicles for the dispatcher.

"Ma'am, I've got law enforcement on the way. In the meantime, I need you to stay on the line and keep me updated on what's happening."

What's happening is that I'm being attacked yet again by some creep who wants me dead.

"We're approaching the intersection of Route 53 and…"

"Box Canyon Road," Henry supplied.

Rose repeated the name for the dispatcher.

At the upcoming intersection a car approaching from the opposite direction had its left turn signal blinking indicating an impending turn in front of them and onto Box Canyon Road.

Racing along the highway at high speed with the blue SUV closing in on them, Henry shoved his hand on the horn and left it there to alert the driver at the intersection that they were about to come through.

Rose was horrified to see that the driver appeared to be distracted by something in the seat beside him and he was beginning the turn without looking in front of him.

Henry lifted his foot from the accelerator as the driver continued farther into his turn until he finally looked up and saw the truck headed toward him. In what must have been a panicked reaction, the man irrationally hit the brakes and came to a stop mid-turn.

The assailant in the SUV roared up behind them.

Bang!

A bullet struck Rose's side mirror.

Henry swerved around the driver who'd stopped in front of them and the sudden movement made Rose drop her phone. There was an upcoming curve in the road with no way to see if someone was heading right for them. *Please, Lord, help us avoid a head-on collision,* Rose frantically prayed while hanging on to her seat with both hands.

Henry made it past the stopped driver and back into their own lane.

"Grab your phone and see if 9-1-1 dispatch can tell us the ETA for our responding officers."

"They're right here," Rose said, spotting flashing red and blue lights on the road up ahead.

Bang! Bang!

The gunman fired two more shots, one of them clipping the side of the truck close to Rose, before the driver started backing off. In her cracked mirror, Rose could see the blue SUV making a wide U-turn and then accelerating away along the highway behind them. She reached down to the floorboard to retrieve her phone.

"You okay?" Henry asked, taking his foot off the accelerator and pulling to the side of the road before coming to a stop.

"Yeah." Rose figured she must be in shock since she felt numb rather than afraid. She put her phone to her ear. "Are you still there?" she asked.

"Yes," the dispatcher replied. "Update me on what's happening."

"The attacker in the blue SUV is now headed southbound. We're parked by the side of the road and we can see the approaching officers."

"Okay, remain with your vehicle until you speak with one of the officers."

Rose turned to look at Henry, practically drinking in his disciplined composure and taking comfort from it. That had to come from the military and private security work he'd dedicated most of his life to, and she was grateful for it. This was not the smart-alecky guy she'd known years ago who wouldn't take anything seriously. And he was not a man at all inclined to pursue a criminal lifestyle like his parents had done. Rose could hardly believe she'd ever thought those things about him.

"It'll be okay," Henry said as two sheriffs' deputy patrol cars sped pass them in pursuit of the assailant SUV. An approaching police cruiser slowed and crossed the highway to park in front of them.

"Don't be discouraged," Henry added, reaching over to brush Rose's hair from her face and tuck it behind her ear. "Sometimes it takes a while to stop the bad guys, but that doesn't mean it can't be done."

Tears began to fall from Rose's eyes as her feeling of numbness gave way to fear and discouragement despite Henry's attempt at a pep talk.

It took her a moment to realize her tears also represented other emotions, feelings that were much more tender. The combination of toughness and kind consideration that Henry Walsh had consistently shown Rose was getting past her defenses. Beyond the worry and frustration and fear for her life that had her trembling with the rush of adrenaline, she was beginning to truly care about Henry Walsh.

That was a dangerous situation in a completely different way. It was dangerous for her heart, when Henry moved on with whatever life he decided to live, wherever his eventual plans might take him.

Henry gently brushed away Rose's tears and kissed her on the forehead and again lightly on her cheek just as the cop walked up to their truck. Was Henry feeling it, too? It seemed as if he was. What might that mean for their future?

Or could this be only a temporary feeling in response to the life-threatening experiences they'd gone through together?

The officer wasn't Kris Volker, unfortunately. Rose and Henry got out of the truck to talk to him. After assuring him they weren't injured, they described what had happened.

A transmission came across the cop's radio that sounded like Henry's friend Dylan Ruiz. "Dispatch, SD-615. I've lost sight of the blue SUV. There are several places where it could have turned off. I'm going to drive around and see if I can find it."

"Copy, SD-615."

"Dylan will put in a good effort to find him," Henry said, moving closer to Rose and wrapping an arm around her shoulders.

"I know," she said, leaning into him.

She would try hard to take Henry's advice and not let herself get discouraged. But the truth was there were paved roads, private roads, logging roads and fire roads all over the place. That SUV could be anywhere. Dylan likely wouldn't find it and the attacker or attackers would get away again.

Right now she had way more questions than answers. But like Henry, she could be strong and determined. She leaned closer against him and he tightened his hug. *Thank You, Lord, that I don't have to go through this alone.*

"When you're ready, we'll need to go into town so I can take an official statement," the police officer said.

Rose nodded. "Of course." She supposed she was as ready as she was ever going to be. "Let's go." She allowed herself to hope that Chief Ellis and his officers had made some headway by now in figuring out the identities of the criminals who were so determined to get to her.

* * *

"Maybe you should stay at the ranch and rest today," Henry said to Rose over a cup of coffee the following morning. "You've been through a lot these past three days."

Yesterday afternoon had been spent at the police station where he and Rose had given their statements. Of course a vehicle matching the description of the SUV had been reported stolen earlier in the day, so identifying the owner of the vehicle would not take them any closer to identifying the attackers.

Both Henry and Rose had noted their impression that there must have been two people in the SUV, though they never got a clear look at them. Someone obviously had to be driving while someone else was firing the bullets that struck the passenger side of Henry's truck. While they were at the station, a detective had shown them a half dozen new mug shots forwarded by law enforcement agencies from around the Montana-Idaho region in hopes of getting a name for the two attackers, but that had been a bust. After that, they'd dropped off Henry's truck to get the broken window and mirror fixed.

Rose had been quiet after Bennie met them in town at the auto-repair shop and drove them back to the ranch. But later, after dinner, she'd voiced her desire to talk to her parents in person as soon as possible.

Now, caught in a beam of morning sunlight shining through the kitchen window, she looked at Henry and shrugged in response to his suggestion that she should hang out at the ranch for a while. "If I spend the day hiding here, it will just take that much longer to get to the bottom of who's attacking me and why."

"Sounds like you're still not counting on the cops to take care of that."

She shook her head and took a sip of coffee. "The police are obviously doing everything they can to track down the assailants," she said, "but after talking to the cops yesterday, it's clear they're focused on finding the thugs who have been attacking me. That makes sense. It's their job. But nobody seemed interested in looking deeper into Gabe Kraft's life to get a handle on why someone's targeted me. Maybe if they concentrate on physically tracking down the attackers and I try to figure out what message Kraft left for me in his files, then together we can wrap this up and I can go back to my normal life."

Henry broke eye contact for a moment, afraid what he felt for Rose might be visible in his eyes. He was a little alarmed at the reminder that she intended to leave Cedar Lodge and go away to college.

But, he reminded himself, once the ranch was fully restored he planned on leaving town, too. Returning to Cedar Lodge had stirred up painful memories of his youth and his neglectful parents. At least he'd had his grandmother and this ranch she'd called home. She'd welcomed him every time he came for a visit and he only now realized he probably could have moved here permanently during his turbulent teen years if he'd just asked. But at the time it had been important for him to feel as if he didn't need anybody.

"After we talk to my parents, I want to try and speak with Dora Ross and Thomas Conway and see what their connection was with Kraft," Rose said after a couple more sips of coffee. "Maybe they know what that code on their files means."

"How do you know Dora and Thomas?"

"About five years ago I picked up a part-time job at a

grocery store to earn money working weekends and Dora was employed there, too. We weren't buddies or anything like that, but she was a nice, friendly person. Thomas Conway manages his dad's car dealership and I met him when he came to the insurance office where I work to do some price comparison for property and liability insurance for his dad's business. He called me after our meeting and we met for a coffee, but it quickly became apparent we didn't have much in common so that was the end of it."

"Nice guy?" Henry asked, feeling an unreasonable hint of jealousy.

"Charming, I'd say," Rose said thoughtfully, "which isn't the same thing."

"No, it's not." Lots of dangerous people were skilled at turning up the charm when it benefited them.

"You're not especially charming," Rose said with a teasing smile. "But I don't hold that against you."

"Thanks, I guess." What did that mean, exactly? Henry was out of practice when it came to interpreting personal comments about him made by attractive women. "Have you already contacted Dora or Thomas?" he asked, quickly changing the subject.

"No." Rose got up and set her empty coffee mug in the sink. Henry did the same thing. "I searched online and found where each of them works," Rose added. "I didn't contact either of them because I was afraid they'd refuse to meet with me if I asked first."

"Good thinking." Back in the day Rose had been known for focusing on a task and then getting it done no matter the challenges in her way. Like when she convinced unruly high school kids to help clean up the parking lot at a hamburger stand near their high school that the students frequented. It was good to see her bold determination was still working for her. Hopefully it wouldn't put her in danger.

"Can we get going?" Rose prompted, causing Henry to realize he'd been gazing at her a little too long.

"Yep." He walked out of the house and onto the porch ahead of her so he could take a look around and make sure the area was secure. Then they headed for the old truck that he'd bought for Viv to use. He'd already let Viv know he needed to borrow it temporarily until he could get his own vehicle back from the repair shop.

Rose gave him general directions to her parents' house and they started down the long ranch drive toward the county highway. They passed through Cedar Lodge, and a few miles beyond the edge of town they reached a small community surrounded by forest with a country store, a diner and a couple of other businesses at the crossroads. From there they headed up a hill until Rose finally told him to slow down and then pointed at a two-story home with a boat on one side, a camper trailer on the other and two late-model vehicles in the driveway.

Not exactly what Henry had expected to see, given that Rose's parents had borrowed money from a loan shark *twice*. He supposed he'd imagined them destitute. But maybe this was exactly what he should have expected. Glancing around the neighborhood, it was clear they had kept up with the Joneses despite not being able to afford it. People like them would have been an easy target for a loan shark like Gabe Kraft.

Rose started to get out of the truck and Henry gestured at her to stay seated. "Hang on a sec," he said, taking a good look around before indicating that it looked safe to exit the pickup. He wanted to believe that using Viv's truck would keep them hidden from the bad guys, but with Rose's safety at stake, he wouldn't take any chances.

"Do your parents know we're coming?" he asked.

"Yeah, I texted my mom on the way over. She's the only one here. Dad is at work."

They headed for the front door.

Rose's parents had interacted with Gabe Kraft several times over the years. Maybe they'd picked up information while talking to the loan shark that would help them get to the bottom of the current situation and figure out the reason for the attacks on Rose. There had now been multiple major attempts to kidnap or kill her. The longer this went on, the more likely it was that she would get seriously hurt, or worse.

EIGHT

Rose's mother opened the front door and stood for a moment wringing her hands before wrapping her arms around her daughter for a lingering hug.

Henry didn't want to be rude, but he nevertheless nudged the two woman forward so all three of them could get inside the house and close the door behind them. He didn't want Rose exposed to anyone who might be hidden outside watching and waiting for her to show up here so they could make another attempt to kidnap or kill her.

"Dad's going to be so sorry he missed you," Mrs. Balfour said as they walked into the living room.

"I almost didn't tell you about the terrible things that have been happening because I didn't want you to worry."

"And when you did let us know, you told us about them by text," her mom muttered, sounding unhappy about it.

"I didn't want to actually talk with you about it because I didn't want us to get emotional and fall to pieces." Rose smiled faintly at her mother. "And I avoided coming over here until now because I didn't want to risk putting you and Dad in danger. But things have gotten bad enough that I have to make some tough decisions. Coming over here was one of them."

Mrs. Balfour took a steadying breath. "Well, I'm just glad you're here."

Rose turned to make the introduction between Henry and her mom, Liz.

"Henry Walsh." Mrs. Balfour repeated his name as they sat down. "That name sounds familiar."

Henry braced himself for a comment about his parents. Their arrests had made it into the local news on more than one occasion back in the day. Although as a minor Henry's name had been left out of public reports, Cedar Lodge had still been a very small town back then, and lots of people would have known about Henry's connection to them, anyway.

"I think you two were in the same grade in high school, weren't you?" Mrs. Balfour asked Rose. "I'm fairly sure I heard you mention his name a few times when you were talking to your friends."

Henry's heart did a two-step at the thought that Rose had talked about him to someone all those years ago.

"Mom, I need to discuss something with you and I know you're not going to like it." Rose's cheeks reddened as she quickly changed the subject.

Mrs. Balfour, a slightly chubby woman with short medium-brown hair that was graying at the temples, sat back in a chair as if bracing herself for the information. "Go ahead."

Rose sighed heavily and Henry began to feel exceedingly awkward.

"I know you and Dad borrowed money from Gabe Kraft a second time, shortly before he died."

Mrs. Balfour's lips tightened and she looked away from her daughter. "And how would you know that?"

"I searched through some of Kraft's files in his house. What did you need the money for?"

"Your father and I deserve to enjoy life and have nice things as much as anybody else." Mrs. Balfour crossed her arms defensively over her chest. "And why did Kraft give you his house? Have you figured that out yet?"

"I think he wanted me to find information that would lead to his likely killer if he was murdered. That's my best guess." Rose shook her head. "But the loan, Mom, *why* did you and Dad do that again after all we went through to get your previous loan with Gabe Kraft paid off?"

Henry wondered if Rose had taken that extra job at the grocery store she'd mentioned in order to help her parents pay off that first loan.

"Dad and I didn't ask you to bail us out again," Mrs. Balfour said defiantly. At the same time she brushed quickly forming tears from her eyes.

"You didn't ask me for help because Kraft died soon after you took out the loan. The debt vanished at that point, obviously, but now I'm concerned you'll take out another loan from someone else." Rose cleared her throat. "I think you and Dad should seek counseling to help figure out why you make the same mistakes over and over again."

"The debt wasn't erased." Mrs. Balfour replied so softly that Henry barely heard her.

"What?" Rose leaned closer to her mom. "What are you talking about?"

Mrs. Balfour uncrossed her arms and rested her hands on her knees. "Your dad and I heard that Gabe Kraft had been murdered and we assumed we were off the hook for the loan. But then a short time after the murder, a different man contacted us and said he'd be taking over the business. He gave us directions on where to drop off the first cash payment to him and said he'd call us every week with updated directions on where to leave the next payment. The night he first contacted us, a brick was thrown through our bedroom window in the middle of the night. I suppose that was a message that he knows where we live and we'd better pay up."

"Mom, why didn't you tell me about this?"

Her mother arched an eyebrow. "Your father and I didn't want to get a lecture from you about how we shouldn't have taken out the loan in the first place."

Henry resisted the urge to shake his head as he empathized with what Rose must be feeling. It sounded as if her parents hadn't learned anything from their experiences, and yet Rose would likely continue to feel compelled to help them.

"Did you at least call the police?" Rose asked, her face ashen.

"We were afraid to. This new loan shark threatened to hurt us if we did."

"But the cops could trace his phone number and catch the guy."

Liz Balfour shook her head. "It's a different number every time and it always appears as if he's calling from somewhere outside of the country."

"Phone spoofing technology," Henry said. "A way to make a phone call appear as if it's originating from someplace other than where it's truly coming from." Henry turned to Mrs. Balfour. "I understand you're afraid," he said gently, "but you can't go on living like this. Let me see if I can do anything to help. I promise, I'll be subtle about it."

Rose stood and walked over to her mother to offer her a comforting hug.

Henry respected her for responding to her mother in such a gracious, forgiving way.

"I think you should trust Henry and let him help you," Rose said to her mom after their embrace ended. "I trust him completely."

Henry couldn't help feeling a little bit proud hearing her say that.

Mrs. Balfour agreed to talk to her husband about allowing Henry to help them.

"We need to go now, Mom," Rose said. "There were a couple of other people whose names I came across in Gabe Kraft's files and I want to talk to them."

"Be careful," her mom told Rose and Henry before they left.

"So, you trust me completely," Henry said to Rose with a grin once they were out the door and safely back in his truck.

"Don't let it go to your head," she retorted, unable to keep from laughing.

"Too late, it already has."

But within moments the mood shifted and neither of them was laughing anymore. It was time to be vigilant because they had to drive back through town, and hopefully the bad guys wouldn't spot them. Henry wouldn't rest easy until they returned to the ranch. And even then, after the shooting on the highway, he was concerned the assailants might have somehow figured out where Rose was staying by perhaps following them without being detected at some point.

"Who do you want to talk to first and where exactly will we find them?" Henry asked.

"Dora Ross. She works at Super Mart."

"All right." Henry headed in that direction while thinking about how he could help Rose's parents. Finding out they were currently in a threatening situation was obviously painful for Rose. She'd already been through so much, and it didn't look as if things were going to get easier for her anytime soon.

"I don't mean to upset you," Rose told the petite red-haired woman standing across from her in the Super Mart salad dressing and condiments aisle. "But the situation has become very dangerous for me and any information you could offer would be helpful."

Dora shifted her worried gaze from Rose to Henry, who stood a couple feet away. The three of them had stepped into an aisle momentarily free of shoppers so they could have a private conversation.

After offering a friendly greeting and walking with Rose and Henry until they could find a place to chat, Dora's demeanor had drastically changed when Rose introduced the topic of Gabe Kraft. "I don't know why you think I had any connection with that man," Dora said. "He was a criminal."

Rose pulled her phone from her pocket, tapped the screen a few times and then showed Dora the photo she'd taken of the document in Gabe Kraft's file cabinet with Dora's name and the strange mixture of numbers and letters that made no obvious sense. "I'm sorry, Dora, but we found this inside Kraft's house. I'd like to know what this code means."

Dora's blue eyes filled with tears and then her expression turned defiant. "Why did that creep leave you his house?" she demanded. "Were you involved with him somehow?" The sneer she added to the term *involved* clearly implied she thought Rose might have had a close personal relationship with the loan shark. "People all over town are wondering what that weird turn of events is all about," she added snidely.

"I wasn't involved with him." Rose fought to keep her tone neutral despite being chilled by Dora's sudden change in demeanor. "I think Kraft suspected his life was in danger and hoped if something happened I'd look through his files and identify his killer."

"Well, I didn't kill him," Dora said, "and I don't know why he had my name written down in his files."

"Could you at least tell me what this code refers to?" Rose pressed.

Dora shrugged. "I have no idea. Now I need to get back to work. Please leave me alone."

She turned and stalked away. Rose considered following after her to try asking for her help one more time. But then Henry stepped up to Rose and reassuringly rested his hand on her shoulder. "If you don't press too hard, she might have a change of heart and be willing to answer your questions later."

He was right, of course. And it wasn't as if Rose could force Dora to talk to her. Nor would she want to.

"While I was showing Dora that picture of the paper we'd found with her name and the code on it, I thought of something I've wondered about before. If the assailants are attacking me because of something in Gabe Kraft's files, why didn't they just go into the house and steal them? The house has been unoccupied for roughly ten months."

Henry shook his head. "I don't know. Maybe they broke in and looked at the files but couldn't make sense of them or couldn't find some specific thing they were looking for."

"There's also the possibility that the files we found aren't connected to anything significant at all," Rose said, her heart sinking.

"It won't help to fixate on what we don't know right now," Henry said, lightly squeezing her shoulder before removing his hand. "Let's go talk to the other person whose name you recognized, Thomas Conway. You said he works at Cedar Lodge Auto Sales, right? That's only four blocks away."

"Okay," Rose said softly, her thoughts turning to the people who were forced to face terrible situations in their life without someone like Henry to help them and keep their sprits boosted. *Thank You, Lord, for Your provision and blessings.* Rose considered herself a helpful person, but she realized that going forward in life she could probably do a little bit more for others who needed assistance or encouragement.

They walked out of the grocery store, with Henry keeping a close eye on their surroundings, as usual. Rose also scanned the area. An attack could be launched at any time, virtually anywhere. She knew that only too well.

"It's outrageous that you've had to endure the assaults that I've learned about in the news," Thomas Conway said to Rose with a sympathetic shake of his head. "I'm so sorry it's happening to you."

"Thank you," Rose said. Thomas was a nice man and Rose had enjoyed that one coffee date with him, but their interests and values just hadn't converged. "I appreciate you agreeing to talk with us."

"Of course."

Rose and Thomas sat at a picnic table in a grassy corner at the juncture of the car dealership's sales office and repair shop. Henry remained standing so he could more easily keep an eye on their surroundings and any potential danger. Thomas had made it clear he couldn't speak frankly inside the building where the owner—his father—and his coworkers would certainty eavesdrop.

"I need to talk to you about Gabe Kraft," Rose began, hoping that the mention of the loan shark wouldn't cause Thomas to end the conversation like Dora had.

"That's what I expected you to say after you told me you weren't here to buy a car."

"Seriously?"

Thomas nodded. "For one thing, Kraft did will you his house and that's been a hot topic of conversation all over town. I also read somewhere that you were a witness in his murder trial. And now, well, here you are."

"And you have a connection to Gabe Kraft?" Rose asked.

Thomas gave her a level look. "You're here because you know I do."

He wasn't going to try to hide his tie to the loan shark. That was a relief. "So, Gabe Kraft loaned you money at his customary ridiculously high interest rate and then threatened you with bodily harm if you didn't pay him on time, correct?"

"No." Thomas shook his head. "He blackmailed me."

Rose's stomach dropped. *"Blackmail?"* She exchanged glances with Henry, who was close enough to hear him.

"Yes." Thomas ran a hand through his dark blond hair. "He had photos of me with a woman other than my wife."

Rose hadn't realized Thomas was married, though now she noticed the gold wedding band on his finger.

"My wife, Sandy, and I separated for a few months shortly after our wedding, which was almost two years ago." Thomas crossed his arms and leaned forward, resting his elbows on top of the picnic table. "My wife had just turned twenty-two when we got married. And I was nearly ten years older than her. After three months of married life, she told me she thought she'd gotten married too young. She missed frequently going out with her friends."

Thomas uncrossed his arms and leaned back a little. "I should have anticipated that since she was so young, but I didn't. I just knew I loved her and wanted to spend the rest of my life with her." He looked directly at Rose and the emotion she saw in his eyes made her heart ache for him.

"I really believed our marriage was over, because Sandy had said that it was. Then, like an idiot, I started drinking to temporarily ease the pain after she moved out and I threw myself into the arms of another woman. I didn't genuinely care about the other woman and she definitely didn't really care about me."

"And Kraft got pictures of you with this other woman?"

"Yeah. Nothing horribly salacious. Just the two of us outside a bar, kissing fairly exuberantly." He stared in the distance for a few seconds before turning back to Rose. "Sandy came back to me." Thomas's voice caught and he paused again for a moment. "She said she realized that she didn't want to go back to partying with her friends. That after several nights out with her single buddies, she realized the value of having a loving husband waiting for her at home."

Rose nodded at him, imagining the regret he must have felt for trying to ease his former heartbreak by drinking and racing out to find a new girlfriend.

"I was afraid to tell Sandy about the other woman. So I didn't. I did, however, stop drinking. And I made several good decisions in the wake of that choice."

"How did Kraft happen to take those pictures?" Henry asked.

Rose winced inwardly at the insensitivity of the question. But at the same time she did wonder how Kraft had found his blackmail victim.

Thomas gestured toward the dealership building. "In a

small town people tend to think of someone who owns a car dealership as being rich. From the time I was a teenager, I wanted to get attention by being the cool rich kid, even though it's my dad who's wealthy and I had to work for any money he gave me. Something I appreciate now, because I do have a decent work ethic.

"Anyway, like an idiot I drew a lot of attention to myself at the clubs in town and I drank too much and overshared the details of the breakup of my marriage with anybody willing to listen. Combine the juicy gossip about my personal life with the perception that I had a lot of money and you have a recipe for a blackmailer to come sniffing around. Which is obviously what happened."

"Rest assured we won't share the details of your personal life with anyone," Henry interjected.

Rose was glad he'd said something about that because she hadn't thought to mention it.

"Thanks. I'm actually benefiting from talking about this with you. I need the practice of confessing my stupidity because I've made up my mind to tell my wife about the temporary girlfriend and what a fool I was. I don't want to keep it secret from her any longer, and word of it will inevitably make its way to her eventually. I really do love Sandy and I want our marriage to be strong and based on truth."

"Have you tried praying for help with that?" Rose asked.

"I haven't prayed since I was a kid," Thomas said with a laugh.

Rose smiled at him. "You can start again anytime."

Thomas's expression shifted and he looked as if he were seriously considering her suggestion.

"Would we be right to assume the demand for payment to keep your secret ended when Gabe Kraft died?" Henry asked.

"Oh, no," Thomas said. "That's another reason why I'm telling you my story right now. I want the creep who is continuing the blackmail demands and threats to be caught. I hope you two can help make that happen."

"You could report it to the police," Rose suggested.

"No way." Thomas shook his head emphatically. "And if you try to report it to the police for me, I'll deny everything."

Rose found herself even angrier at Kraft for what he'd put people through. It had been especially cruel of him to prey on people in ways that would make them too ashamed or embarrassed to ask law enforcement for help.

"When Gabe Kraft originally contacted me for blackmail money, he not only threatened to expose my relationship with the other woman to my wife, he said he'd have someone hurt both myself and my wife if I contacted the police. And then he told me he knew who set the Boyd Mansion fire that killed that poor homeless person who'd been staying inside it. He said the people who set the fire were paying him big money to keep his mouth shut so they wouldn't get charged with arson and murder because they were smart enough to be afraid of him." Thomas shrugged. "I don't know if that's really true, or he just thought it would impress and scare me."

This was unexpected information. Rose exchanged glances with Henry.

"I need to get back to work." Thomas stood and Rose did, too.

"Thank you for your time," she said.

Thomas nodded. "I wish you well with your investigation."

Rose and Henry returned to the truck while Thomas walked back inside the dealership.

"I don't remember the Boyd Mansion fire being classified as arson," Rose said. "I remember there were a few unsubstantiated rumors going around that it had been intentionally set, but everything I read about it said it was an accidental fire, likely caused by the homeless person who'd broken into the building and was staying there."

"This whole thing is strange," Henry said as he started the truck. "I suspect the alphanumeric codes written on some of the files indicated who Kraft was targeting for blackmail as opposed to his normal loan-sharking victims. Now I want to talk to Kris and Dylan, unofficially at first, and see what they think about all of this. And at the same time maybe they could put together a plan for helping your parents."

Rose nodded. "Good idea."

Things were getting very complicated and talking it over with the cops would be beneficial. Maybe it would lead to the end of the criminal enterprise in town that Rose had apparently run up against. It would be a relief to return to a life where she wasn't compelled to constantly look over her shoulder in anticipation of another attack. But for now she would have to remain vigilant.

NINE

Henry drove around to the back of Etta's Family Table, a diner occupying a building that resembled a log cabin, and pulled into a slot in the shadow of a cluster of trees. After the conversation with Thomas Conway, he'd contacted his law enforcement friends and both men had agreed to meet with Henry and Rose.

"Can't be too careful," Rose joked nervously, taking a breath and trying to calm the twisting sensation in her stomach. She was worried about everything, from potential attacks on herself and Henry to the threats leveled against her parents by the unidentified blackmailer.

She slid out of the truck and Henry walked up and wrapped an arm around her. "There aren't many things in this life that we can be certain of," he said, brushing a kiss across her temple and triggering a tingling sensation that overshadowed at least some of her fears, "but we can do our best and we can pray."

"You're right."

Lord, our lives are always in Your loving hands and I know that. Focusing on God instead of her fears helped ease the tension.

"So many times, praying is the *last* thing I think of to

do," Rose commented as they walked around to the diner's front entrance.

"Me, too," Henry said.

He pulled open the door and they stepped inside. The place was busy. She turned to Henry and saw him checking a message on his phone.

A hostess walked up holding some menus. "Just the two of you?"

"Actually, we're meeting a couple of friends who are already in your private banquet room," Henry said, looking up from his phone.

"Oh, sure. Law enforcement officers." The hostess led the way to a room separate from the main dining area. Kris Volker and Dylan Ruiz were seated at a table and both called out greetings as Rose and Henry walked in.

The hostess set down their menus, took their drink orders and then left.

"Thank you for giving up your dinner breaks to meet with us," Rose said.

Henry laughed. "These two aren't giving up anything." He eyed both his old friends. "I have no doubt you'll order food and plan on me picking up the tab."

Both cops grinned in response.

"If Cole Webb were here, you'd have your entire high school gang together," Rose commented.

"We contacted him," Dylan said to her. "He wanted to help, but he's tied up with some kind of paramedic training at the moment."

A server walked in with beverages for Rose and Henry and then took everyone's food orders before leaving.

"I didn't realize they had a banquet room here," Henry commented as the server walked away.

"They don't let just anybody know about it," Kris teased

him. And then more seriously he added, "It seemed best to ensure privacy while we talked."

Henry turned to Rose. "You want to tell them what we learned today?"

"Sure." Rose took a sip of iced tea and then began with a recap of her parents being threatened by an unidentified loan shark.

The cops listened without interruption until she got to the end. Then Kris asked, "Where do they live?"

Rose told him.

"That's past city limits," Kris said with a glance at Dylan. "Your jurisdiction."

"I'll talk to Sheriff Finley about opening an investigation." The deputy turned to Rose. "It might be a good idea to set up a sting operation to catch the perp. Or perps. You said your parents didn't want to report their situation to the authorities. What are the chances they'll work with me if I contact them?"

Rose chewed her bottom lip for a moment. "I think they will after they'd had some time to think about it."

"Contact them this evening and let them know to expect a call from me tomorrow. That should give them enough time to get used to the idea and agree to let me help."

"All right." Rose hoped she was doing the right thing. She glanced nervously at Henry and he reached under the table to take hold of her hand.

"It's your parents' decision whether they want to work with the sheriff's department," Henry said reassuringly. "Nobody is going to force them to do anything."

Rose nodded. "Thanks."

The server brought their food and after everyone began eating Kris asked her, "So what else have you got for us?"

Rose set down her patty melt and told the two law officers what she and Henry had learned regarding Gabe Kraft's blackmailing business. "We know of at least one person who is still being blackmailed and pressured to continue paying. I assume the blackmailer is the same criminal who is keeping Kraft's old loan-sharking business going, but I can't be one hundred percent certain about that. The person claimed Kraft told him the Boyd Mansion fire was arson and that Kraft knew who'd set it ablaze. Kraft claimed he was blackmailing the arsonist. I suppose he mentioned it because he wanted to sound like a criminal to be taken seriously."

"Who is the person being blackmailed?" Kris asked, his attention clearly piqued. "A lot of people suspect that fire was caused by arson but it was labeled accidental due to lack of evidence."

Uncertain how she wanted to respond, Rose turned to Henry.

"We promised not to give away our informant's personal information if he confided in us," Henry said. "And he was emphatic about not wanting to work with the police."

Kris sighed. "It's frustrating when people are too afraid or embarrassed to let us help them."

They continued eating and Rose told the cops her theory that Gabe Kraft had left her his house because he anticipated being murdered and thought Rose would go through all his files and figure out which of his clients was the culprit.

"I was away visiting a friend in Utah when it became public knowledge that I had inherited the house," she said, "and the first attack happened as soon as I arrived back in Cedar Lodge and went to have a look at it. Maybe somebody was afraid of me getting possession of those files."

"If that's the motive for the attacks on you, why didn't

the assailants break into the house and grab the files before you could get to them?" Dylan asked.

"That's what I've wondered," Rose said. "Maybe they assumed they had plenty of time to do that and were taken by surprise when they found out the house had been willed to me. Or maybe they were afraid of getting caught. A neighbor, Curtis Tucker, apparently likes to keep an eye on the place." Rose shook her head. "I don't actually *know* much of anything about this, which is very frustrating."

"Multiple things could be true at once," Kris said thoughtfully. "And it's important not to get tunnel vision. Kraft could have left files with clues for you to find *and* the assailants might not know about it. They might not even consider the files as being of any particular value. It's possible those same assailants simply think you already know something important that they desperately want to keep secret. And maybe you do know something significant and you just don't realize it."

Rose stared at the cop for a moment, stunned by his suggestion that she already knew something that would be important enough for someone to come after her. She had no idea what that could be.

She didn't want to openly dismiss Kris's suggestions because he was being so kind and helpful, but she really thought the motive behind everything was connected to those files. Now that she knew about Kraft's blackmail business, maybe she'd notice something different if she looked through them again. *The pictures.* There were a few actual printed photos mixed in with the files but she hadn't paid much attention to them beyond a quick glance because she'd assumed they were just Kraft's personal photos. She should take a closer look at them. If nothing else, maybe she could find some other blackmail victims and get them some help from the police.

"So what we have," Kris said as they were finishing their meal, "is at least two people who want Rose dead. Possibly a third, since the original attacker was on the phone with an unidentified person before he entered Kraft's house and we don't know if that was the second attacker or somebody else."

"Correct," Rose said.

"And someone, possibly one the aforementioned assailants, has taken over Gabe Kraft's old loan-sharking and blackmailing businesses and is threatening to hurt people if they don't make their payments."

"Correct again," Rose said.

"Meanwhile, Lance Preston is on trial for Gabe Kraft's murder," Dylan interjected. "He's claimed from the beginning that he's been framed. Of course he's going to offer some sort of defense and I'm not saying I believe him. But when you add blackmail to the mix, it brings in a whole other level of people who could have potentially wanted Gabe Kraft dead and then set up Preston to take the fall."

"And when I try to reason through all of that, I only get more confused," Rose said wearily.

Henry squeezed her hand.

Kris nodded sympathetically. "Hopefully, at some point things will begin falling into place and we'll get this figured out."

With their meal finished, Kris and Dylan said their goodbyes and returned to work. Outside, Rose turned her attention to Henry as they strode toward the truck. How could she have ever thought of him as unfocused? Just because he didn't have his future mapped out and important decisions made yet didn't mean he was indecisive or flaky.

She'd been projecting her old impressions of him onto him in the present day and that wasn't fair. She'd also assumed her way of organizing things, with notes and columns and lists, was the only way to go. She'd been wrong. Maybe Henry's way was more intuitive than hers, but he still got his thoughts organized and achieved his goals. Like this meeting, and getting the ball rolling on helping her parents.

"Ready to head back to the ranch?" Henry asked after they were in the truck.

"Let's go by Kraft's house, first," Rose said. "I want to take a quick look through those photos that I didn't spend much time with before. Just to see if it gives us any leads on further blackmail victims."

"We can do that."

"Thanks. I'm so tired of all of this. I want to hurry up and get it figured out and over with."

"I want it over with, too," Henry said. "But we need to be careful. Impatience on our part could turn out to be a serious mistake."

"You're right." Rose didn't want to believe things could get any more dangerous. But they probably could.

"So, no image of anybody setting a fire at the Boyd Mansion?" Henry asked as they left Kraft's house. He didn't feel comfortable having Rose at the house for very long, so he'd encouraged her to take the pictures back to the ranch to examine them more closely there.

"I didn't see anything with a fire in it," Rose replied. "But I did come across some shots of Thomas and the woman I assume was his short-term girlfriend." Rose carried a folder with the photos in it. "I don't know why Kraft chose to print these pictures," she added. "My guess is that he wanted to be able to approach victims and hold up the pictures in front of them. That would certainly get their attention and probably their cooperation when he demanded payment."

"Probably so. Kris mentioned you might already know something that has the attackers worried. Have you been able to think of anything Kraft said or did at any point while you were talking to him that might be important? Or maybe something your parents told you about him?"

"I've tried to think of something, but I can't."

At the end of the driveway Henry was about to turn onto the street when Rose put a staying hand on his arm. "Hold on a minute."

"What?" He liked the touch of her hand but tried not to let his thoughts linger on that.

"Instead of turning left to go back to the ranch, turn right and let's head toward the lake. Do you remember how to get to Buffalo Point?"

"I've never been out there but I can figure it out. That's a very expensive neighborhood. I've never known anybody that wealthy."

"The houses out on the point with the stunning views of the lake and mountains are very expensive, yes," Rose said as Henry made the turn from Gabe Kraft's driveway. "But farther along the shoreline prices are more modest and regular people live there."

"All right. Why are we headed that way?"

"It will be easier to explain after I show you something when we arrive. We won't need to go all the way out to the point. I just want us to drive down a specific lake-access road."

"Okay, I'll wait until we get there for a full explanation. But can you at least tell me what made you suddenly think of going to Buffalo Point?"

She didn't answer right away and Henry glanced over to see her looking at something on her phone. "What is it?" he asked.

"I'm doing some quick research on the Boyd Mansion fire and the poor person who was inside when the place burned down."

"What have you found?"

"This article says the historic mansion had been empty and unoccupied for some time and the deceased, Tony Peale, was a transient who'd likely broken into the building so he could sleep inside it and get out of the cold." Rose looked up from the screen, glanced around and gave Henry updated directions while he drove.

"That's pretty much common knowledge," Henry said.

"There's more. This confirms that it had belonged to Helen Keebler and that she'd recently sold it to a developer from California who'd planned to tear it down. But some locals petitioned the court to put a hold on the development because they believed the house qualified as an historical landmark and should be protected. The court agreed to put a halt to any decisions about the mansion until the situation could be further investigated."

They were stopped at a traffic light and Rose showed Henry a short video with a smartly dressed woman in her late fifties being approached by conservationist protestors. "Helen Keebler?" he asked. He was aware of the Keebler family, a big name in the area, but he didn't remember ever seeing a picture of Helen.

"Yes," Rose confirmed. "There are also images of the same protestors approaching the man who'd intended to buy the mansion from Helen, too."

"Let me guess what happened next," Henry said. "There

was the fire, and since the mansion was destroyed, the sale of the property moved forward and development began."

"Exactly right," Rose said. "This article says there was an inquiry," she continued, looking at her phone, "but the findings were inconclusive. Evidence of lighter fluid was found in the front room on the first floor, but it appeared the homeless man who died had started a fire in there so that wasn't considered proof of arson."

"The Keeblers own a lot of property around here," Henry said as Rose gestured for him to make a turn onto a narrow lane where the rippling waters of Bear Lake were visible ahead. "They've been influential in Cedar Lodge for over a century. I imagine they've got people in place within the fire department and elsewhere who'd block an arson investigation if that's what the family wanted."

"Drive to the edge of the lake and stop right there," Rose said. "Don't turn onto the road that runs along the lakeshore. I want to show you something."

Henry did as she asked. "Wait," he said when she opened her door to get out. "It's too dusky for me to see if anyone's nearby and it might not be safe for you to get out."

"Fine," Rose said, settling back into the truck and closing the door. "But you'll need to pull up a little closer to the edge of the water to get the right view."

Henry nosed the truck forward onto the gravel and grass at the edge of the water. "Okay, now what?"

Rose pointed to the left, where the shoreline curved out to a point of land that jutted into the lake. Lights flickered inside a huge house and a couple of smaller nearby buildings. "Do you know what that is?"

"I bet you're going to tell me," Henry said.

"That would be Helen Keebler's estate." Rose then pointed to her right. "See those much more modest homes?"

Henry glanced at the small bungalows, most appearing to have been built at least a half century ago. "I see the houses," he said. "What is it that you want me to notice?"

"There's nothing for you to notice. It's what I'm going to tell you that might be important." She pointed toward the nearest modest-size house on the right that had a grassy yard leading to the water's edge. "That's where my friend Rhonda lives."

Henry nodded. "Okay."

"About a year and a half ago, Rhonda had knee surgery. She has a young daughter, so she needed people around to help her. For four Saturdays in a row, her husband had to go into work for some special project on a tight deadline. I came to help Rhonda and her daughter on those Saturdays. On two of them, I was in the yard on the grass with Rhonda and little Ceclia and I saw Gabe Kraft drive right up to this juncture here from the direction of the Keebler estate."

"That's odd," Henry said slowly. "I wouldn't have imagined Helen Keebler and Gabe Kraft running in the same circles."

"I thought it was strange, too. But I assumed somebody working at the estate had taken out a loan from him and he was showing up every other week to collect payment. Helen Keebler employs a large staff to care for her house, the grounds, the stables and who knows what else."

"And now you suspect Gabe Kraft was blackmailing Helen Keebler? Or maybe one of her employees who set the fire at the mansion to get it out of the way so the land could be sold for development?"

Rose pressed her lips together and looked at him for a moment. "There's more. I've wondered a lot about why the attacks started when they did. At first I assumed it was because I'd inherited the house, which became public knowledge while I was away in Utah. But just as we were leaving Kraft's house a short while ago, I suddenly remembered talking with Deputy Prosecutor Sloane on a video call while I was in Utah. He'd wanted to prep me for my upcoming testimony.

"He said I'd likely be asked if I was certain it was Gabe Kraft that I'd seen arguing with Lance Preston the day before Kraft was murdered, considering a few years had passed since my parents were involved with him and I'd last seen him. I told Sloane I knew what Kraft looked like more recently because I'd been out here and seen him driving on the road from Helen Keebler's estate."

Henry drew in a deep breath and held it for a few seconds as cold fear for Rose's safety circulated throughout his body. The Keeblers had money and power and they would be a formidable foe to go up against if they were the ones who had targeted Rose.

"So you think Kraft was blackmailing Helen Keebler—or someone she employed—for a substantial amount of money and whoever took over his blackmailing scheme is afraid you'll put the pieces together and ruin everything? Because if you talk to the authorities about a possible pay-off arrangement between Kraft and Keebler, and we can show that Kraft was a blackmailer, that might be enough to have the arson inquiry reopened with an emphasis on looking at whether Helen Keebler had something to do with the fire and Kraft had evidence of it?"

"It seems possible," Rose said softly. "And there's no telling who might have passed along my comments during that video call."

"You mean Sloane?"

"Or someone on his staff, which seems more likely. I had three video calls with him and each time there were members of his staff working or walking by in the background. He routinely had our calls transcribed and a member of the staff would email me a copy. A different person sent it each time. The information could easily have been forwarded to someone who wasn't even in his office at the time of the call."

"So who do you want to talk to about this?" Henry asked after a heavy silence.

"Maybe I should go to Sloane's boss, or the city attorney. Or maybe I should go to Chief Ellis with this." She shook her head. "The Keeblers have influence everywhere. I don't know for certain who I can trust, other than you."

Henry's heart ached with longing to keep Rose safe. He tried to say something to reassure her, but he couldn't seem to put the words together to express how he felt.

"Right now I just want to go back to the ranch," Rose said, prompting Henry to stop gazing at her.

"Right." Henry took a breath to calm his emotions and then maneuvered the truck so he could drive up the lake-access road and back to the highway.

It wasn't fully dark yet, but it was getting close, and clouds were rolling in. Typical of nearly everywhere outside of downtown Cedar Lodge, expanses of thick pine forest stretched along each side of the narrow lane. With no headlights following them and no headlights approaching from the opposite direction, the situation appeared reasonably safe.

Rose turned to him. "What do you think about—"

Bang! Bang! Bang!

Her question was cut off by gunfire coming from the woods, the bullets striking the front tires of the truck and flattening them.

"Hang on!" Henry called out. He shoved his foot hard

on the gas pedal, determined to make it through the ambush without being stopped.

Thump! The swerving, lurching front end of the truck had gotten caught on a large fallen tree limb. Sparks flew up toward the windshield as metal dragged on pavement until the truck's movement slowed to a crawl.

"Henry!"

Henry turned toward Rose and saw the shadowy outline of someone rapidly approaching her side of the truck from the woods. He threw his arm around Rose, pulling her toward him, ready to protect her with his life.

TEN

"**O**pen the door *now* and get out or I'll shoot your boy-friend and then I'll shoot you!" the blond assailant from the original attack screamed at Rose while pressing the barrel of a gun against her window.

"Don't move an inch," Henry said to Rose as he slowly shifted his left hand toward the small of his back and where he'd tucked his gun. His right arm remained wrapped around Rose's shoulder and pulled her even closer.

"Freeze!" the criminal yelled at Henry. "Move that hand near your back again and it will be the last thing you do!" The attacker adjusted his weapon, pointing it at Henry as if about to make good on his threat.

Cold fear churned in the pit of Rose's stomach. How could this be happening? One moment things were fine, and now her world was entirely upended. *Again.*

There was no way she would let Henry get killed because of her. "Let me go," she said, trying to get out from under Henry's arm.

His arm didn't budge. Rose could feel the taut muscles of his body. She knew he was trained and capable if he squared off with the attacker directly. But she was less confident about how things would turn out for him if he put her safety ahead of his own. And she believed that was likely what he would do.

"If this creep was going to just start firing into the truck, he would have done that by now," she said under her breath, hoping the thug couldn't hear her though the rolled-up glass. "He wants to kidnap me, not kill me. If we move slowly, maybe there's something we can do to get out of this."

"I'm not taking any chances with your safety," Henry said, his voice equally quiet. "Don't ask me to."

Fear had triggered a trembling sensation in Rose's chest and now she could feel it spreading throughout her body. Soon her teeth would be chattering, and if she sounded as terrified as she felt, she had no doubt Henry would do whatever he thought necessary to protect her without regard for his own safety. After all they'd been through together, she knew that about him now.

"Get out!" the criminal screamed, shifting his weight from side to side in an agitated fashion that suggested he was on the verge of losing control.

Rose tried to move toward the door and again Henry stopped her.

"You're an experienced hostage negotiator," Rose whispered. "Don't you normally get things moving toward a resolution by giving up something and then asking for a trade? Isn't that how it works?"

"You can't be suggesting that you hand yourself over to this guy."

"We could make it appear as if that's what's happening. And then as soon as I'm out of the truck, you can do whatever you have to do. Attack the guy, shoot at him. Chase him into the woods. Whatever. The longer we sit here and the more anxious he gets, the more likely it is he'll try to kill you before you can grab your gun and fire at him. Plus, for all we know, the other assailant is nearby or about to show up and at that point it'll pretty much all be over."

It felt unreal to find herself giving Henry directions for what to do in the situation, given who he was and what he'd been trained to do. But she could tell that his emotions were getting in the way of his decision. Fear wasn't his problem—his loyalty to Rose was. And she couldn't stand to think of him getting hurt because of that. She also wouldn't let her thoughts linger on what his actions right now might indicate for their future—*if* they had a future. Instead she pressed again against his arm to try to get out of the truck. And this time he let her go.

"Drop to the ground as soon as you can so you're out of the line of fire," Henry said softly. "I'll take care of everything from there."

Rose could do that. Fear alone would likely have her collapsing without even trying. She unlocked the door and began to open it slowly, only to have it yanked from her grasp. The gunman quickly reached for her arm and pulled her out.

Rose's heart felt as if it were pounding at the base of her throat. Her feet hit the ground at an odd angle due to her shakiness and she started to stumble. A drizzling rain was falling. She tried to let herself collapse, but the creep was stronger than he looked and held her up while tightening his grip. He started dragging her toward the woods, but then he made a sudden turn so that they were walking parallel to the road.

It was only now that she could see a vehicle parked up ahead where it was hidden by shadows. No wonder she and Henry hadn't seen it. Was there an accomplice waiting there? What was the plan? Apparently kidnapping her remained their first choice, but where were they going to take her? And what would they do with her once they got there?

Beyond all that, what was happening with Henry right now?

Gulping for breath as her growing terror threatened to choke her, Rose listened for the sound of Henry trailing them, but she couldn't hear him. Tightly holding her arm, the kidnapper walked slightly ahead of Rose, effectively using her as a shield to prevent Henry from taking a shot from behind and attempting to rescue her. The creep hadn't even bothered to try to get Henry's gun from him. Either the criminal really was agitated to the point of not thinking clearly, or he was desperate to grab Rose and get away as quickly as possible.

Lord, help!

There was no way she was getting into the car parked up ahead with this guy. With no idea what Henry was doing, it appeared she would have to save herself. Rose took a deep breath and then bent her knees so she could drop to the ground, hoping that Henry would then get a clear shot at the kidnapper.

The blond criminal stumbled in response, but then righted himself. He bent to grab the back of Rose's shirt and she shoved her elbow behind her as hard as she could. It felt and sounded like she'd hit him square in the nose. He cursed in pain.

Rose twisted from his grasp and kicked the side of his knee. The criminal loosened his grip on her shirt enough for her to wrench free. She ran, not even sure where she was headed other than veering for the cover of the woods.

Bang!

The shot came from the assailant and it sounded close.

At the same time, something hit Rose in the side. Immediately, the point of impact began to burn. Had she been shot?

Bang! Bang! Bang! More shots fired, this time from a different direction.

Was that Henry shooting? Or the second assailant who might be waiting at the car up ahead?

Rose risked slowing to turn around and she saw Henry racing toward the attacker with his gun drawn. The kidnapper had stopped pursuing Rose and was now trying to escape to the car. Rose fell to the ground. Exhausted and with her side hurting, she wanted to be out of the way if more bullets started flying.

Bang! The criminal stopped and spun around just before he reached his vehicle, hurriedly firing one more shot in Henry's direction that appeared to miss its mark. Then the fleeing gunman got into his car and sped away.

"Rose!" Henry veered toward Rose and dropped to the wet ground beside her. Both of them were soaked by the continuing rain. He reached over to brush her soaked bangs from in front of her eyes. "Are you hurt?" he asked gently.

"My side."

Henry grabbed his phone to quickly report the attack and request an ambulance.

By then Rose had steeled up her courage enough to twist around a little and have a look at her injury. "It doesn't appear too bad," she said, moving aside the hole in the fabric and seeing a graze mark rather than a deep bullet wound.

"Let's get out of the rain." Henry wrapped an arm around her uninjured side, helping her up and then back toward his truck.

"That was close," Rose muttered, exhaustion from the adrenaline drop now hitting her.

"Very close," Henry agreed. "Felt like it took forever to

get a clear shot at the jerk without risking shooting you by accident. I don't know what I would have done if something worse had happened to you."

"I feel the same about you," Rose said softly as sirens approached in the distance.

If it was solely her own safety at stake, maybe she would consider relocating away from Cedar Lodge to escape the attacks and remove herself and Henry from danger. But she couldn't just move away and abandon her parents. Maybe once she got her information about Helen Keebler and the Boyd Mansion fire and Gabe Kraft's blackmail business passed along to someone in the justice system, they'd be able to figure out the situation and put a stop to the attacks. Right now Rose felt as if she'd done everything she could possibly do.

"I still think it would be a good idea for you to go to the hospital and get X-rayed," paramedic Cole Webb said to Rose inside the Cedar Lodge police station. "Just to make sure you have no additional injuries."

"Agreed," Henry said, meeting Rose's gaze as she glanced in his direction and hoping he could influence her to take Cole's advice.

"If it feels like something is seriously wrong later, then I will," Rose said, turning back to Cole. "The last thing I want to do right now is waste my time hanging around an emergency room when I don't need to be there."

"It's your decision," Cole said.

"Yes, it is," Rose grumbled. But then almost immediately, as Cole stood to leave, Rose reached out to grab his hand. "I'm sorry, I didn't mean to snap at you. I'm just tired and cranky and angry over everything that's been happening."

The medic gave her hand a squeeze before letting go.

"Oh, Rose, you've been cranky since high school. I've never held it against you."

Henry enjoyed the look of astonishment that appeared on Rose's face before she burst out in laughter. "I'm not cranky. I just speak plainly and I've never understood why that gets under some people's skin."

She did speak plainly and Henry liked that. His parents and their low-life friends could turn on the charm like flicking a switch when they wanted to get something from someone. It was comforting to him to be around a woman who spoke the same way all the time and didn't indulge in false charm to manipulate people.

"I'll see y'all later," Cole said with a broad grin before he picked up his first-aid bag and headed for the police station exit.

Cole had been on the ambulance that responded to the shooting. Kris had been ahead of him, along with officers in three other patrol cars. After making contact with Rose and Henry, Kris had directed the other cops to search for the gunman and they'd taken off looking for the vehicle that Rose and Henry had described.

Rose had climbed into Cole's ambulance at the scene so he could check her injury. He had confirmed that the bullet had scraped off a layer of her skin while Henry had waited anxiously in the rain, hoping that her injury wasn't worse than it appeared.

Cole, who admitted to being a bit of a worrier when it came to a person's health, had followed Rose and Henry to the police station with the intention of convincing Rose to get X-rays taken of her ribs, but she obviously wasn't going for that.

Henry watched Cole disappear from view and then turned to Kris. The only person missing from the circle of childhood friends, Deputy Dylan, was still out searching for the gunman who remained at large. All three of Henry's old friends had shown up to help when he and Rose were in trouble, and he took a moment to appreciate how blessed he was to have them in his life.

He couldn't help wondering what his life would have been like if he'd returned to Montana following his military service like the others had done. Would he have a cozy, settled life like they all did now? Would he have a young son, like Kris Volker had? A pang in his heart took him by surprise as he realized how much he wanted what they had.

Someday, he told himself.

Rose and Henry settled in with Kris in his office and gave him the information he needed to complete his report. Quickly moving on to the bigger picture of the possible reason behind all of the attacks, Rose took the opportunity to tell him about having seen Gabe Kraft in the vicinity of the Keebler estate. She went on to explain her theory that Kraft might have been blackmailing Helen Keebler or one of her employees.

"And you think someone inside the deputy prosecutor's office heard your conversation with Sloane and told someone in the Keebler camp about what you had seen?" Kris clarified.

"It makes sense," Henry commented, growing increasingly concerned for Rose's safety.

Kris leaned back in his chair. "I have to push back on this a little," he said. "Think about it, why would Helen Keebler risk being convicted of arson? We can set aside the murder for the moment because it's possible whoever set the fire didn't realize there was anyone inside the mansion. But Helen Keebler is already wealthy. Why take that kind of risk?"

"Maybe she wants to be even wealthier," Henry countered. "For some people, greed knows no bounds."

"Or maybe the purchaser of that land, the developer or one of their representatives, was staying at the Keebler estate and that's who Kraft was meeting with," Rose suggested. "Maybe the developer was willing to commit arson because the potential amount of money to be made in developing that piece of land is so great. Plenty of people are moving here from around the country. All of them need housing so there's lots of money to be made."

"Everything we're suggesting includes a lot of *maybes*," Kris said. "Meanwhile, there's no open arson investigation for me to pursue. The fire was deemed accidental. I talked with Chief Ellis about this after we all met at the restaurant. He told me it's going to take facts and proof or possibly the sworn testimony of an eye witness for him to get authorization for an arson investigation. A deep dive into a potential connection between Helen Keebler and the Boyd Mansion fire would require additional solid evidence, as well."

Rose slumped in her chair, looking disappointed. Henry could imagine how she felt. Actually, he considered how she felt fairly often. For several terrifying moments as she was being dragged toward the woods by the attacker, Henry had been overwhelmed thinking about the stark terror she must have been experiencing. With emotions settling down somewhat now that they were safe at the police station, his thoughts about her were beginning to clear.

He'd let himself get drawn in too closely to Rose. Yes, he did want a home life someday like Kris and Cole and Dylan had. But that was a plan for the future. He was still too unsettled at the moment, still uncertain about what he wanted to do with the next phase of his life. He realized he'd been back in town long enough to know he didn't really care what people in general thought about him or whether they remembered his thieving, drug-dealing parents. And if anyone still thought he was a person of questionable character like his mother and father had been, well, that person would be ill-informed and a fool.

But he did care what Rose thought about him. He cared too much.

It was his own fault for giving in to the pull of attraction he'd felt for Rose and letting himself feel connected with her in a way he had never felt with any woman before. He enjoyed his friendship with her and their shared sense of humor. Their deeper discussions and the feeling that the air nearly sparkled when he was around her added enjoyment to his life that he truly appreciated.

But indulging in all of that was not a good idea and he needed to knock it off. He couldn't offer her a future. She had plans for her life, plans to finally get away from Cedar Lodge and experience something new, which she'd long wanted to do. Henry wouldn't take that from her.

Besides, who said she wanted any kind of serious relationship with him? How much of her attraction to him was because he was willing to protect her while she was in danger? His skills might at times make him appear heroic, but he was no hero. And any attraction to him based on that would only be temporary.

"I'm worn out," Rose said. "Physically tired and emotionally drained. I just want somebody to unravel what's happening, figure out who wants me kidnapped or dead and why, and then I want them to bring an end to it all immediately."

"I can't promise to make it all end immediately," Kris said, "but I'll do everything I can to get this resolved as quickly as possible."

"Still no leads on the identities of the creeps who keep attacking us?" Henry asked his friend.

"We've sent bulletins throughout the region with written descriptions and composite images of the perps, but so far no response. You've already seen all the images we have of anyone we're aware of who comes close in appearance. Seems evident the criminals aren't locals. We could still get a response from a distant law enforcement agency giving us names for the attackers. We aren't giving up yet."

"Thanks," Henry said. He turned to Rose. "Ready to go?"

"Sure. How are we going to get back to the ranch? Shall we get a rideshare?" The damaged truck with its front tires shot out had been towed to a garage for repairs.

"I can take you home," Kris offered.

Home. The word and the idea struck at Henry more deeply than he wanted it to. Where exactly was his home and where did he want it to be? Cedar Lodge or somewhere else? He still didn't know.

Rain was still falling as they stepped outside and headed toward Kris's patrol car. With Rose walking close beside him, Henry nearly wrapped his arm around her, but at the last moment he caught himself and shoved his hands into his pockets instead. He wrestled his attention away from Rose and focused on their surroundings, almost hoping one of the creeps would attack right now so he and Kris could go after them.

Henry needed to go back to thinking like a soldier, not some lovesick fool. He wanted to keep Rose safe and bring an end to whatever criminal endeavor was operating in Cedar Lodge and making her their target. Then he and Rose could both move on to whatever came next in their lives. Separately. That would be best for both of them. He was certain of it.

ELEVEN

"Henry's friend Deputy Ruiz is very nice," Liz Balfour said to her daughter the following morning over the phone. "I was a little unhappy when he first contacted me, but now I want to see the lowlife who's been threatening your dad and me put into jail. My thanks to you and Henry for getting this going."

"You're welcome, Mom." Rose stood in the kitchen at the ranch, stretching her body as she spoke with her mother, trying to loosen all the muscles that were sore after last night's attack without putting any pressure on her injury. She'd started the call by letting her mom know there'd been another assault but that she was all right, and then she'd quickly steered the conversation toward a different topic before her mother could get too worried.

"So, does Dylan have an actual plan in place yet?" Rose asked.

"Yes. Your dad and I have a payment due today. When the loan shark calls with directions on where to leave the cash payment this time, I'm supposed to immediately call Dylan with the details. He'll set up a stakeout at the payment location and hopefully catch the guy."

"You and Dad be careful," Rose warned.

"Worry about yourself instead of us, honey. We'll be

okay," Liz said before offering a warm goodbye and dis-connecting.

Viv had left plates of breakfast warming in the oven and the rumbling in Rose's stomach prompted her to go check on it. In the same text letting her know that break-fast was ready whenever she wanted it, Viv had also said that she and Bennie were going into town for a while and that Henry had gotten a very early start on his fencing proj-ect this morning.

Rose sighed heavily while pouring herself more coffee. Henry had avoided her after they returned to the ranch last night. Even in Volker's patrol car on the way here, he hadn't had much to say to Rose and she'd wondered if something was wrong. In the end, she'd decided that, like her, he was probably tired and trying to emotionally recover from the attack. Both of them had a lot to think about, especially when it came to figuring out how to move forward with their theory on Helen Keebler and the fire at the mansion and how that fit together with everything else going on.

Rose moved slowly toward the oven, still not feeling completely awake despite the phone call and the coffee she'd already sipped. Without any specific leads to follow up on, she planned to spend the day looking through the photos she'd taken from Kraft's house. Nothing had leaped out at her when she'd first glanced at them yesterday, but maybe this morning she'd notice something that she'd pre-viously missed.

She grabbed a potholder and opened the oven door to pull out one of two plates covered with tinfoil. She took her plate to the table and pulled off the covering, taking in the sight and delicious scent of breakfast enchiladas and spicy fried potatoes. She'd just grabbed some cutlery and a paper napkin when she heard the front door open and close followed by the sound of bootsteps on the wooden floor headed her direction.

Henry came into view, wearing jeans and a muscle-hugging black T-shirt. He pulled off his cowboy hat to hang it on a peg on the wall and then wiped the sweat from his brow with his forearm.

"Good morning," Rose said brightly, happy to see him.

"Good morning."

"This is perfect timing. I was just about to eat break-fast, too." She smiled at him as he headed toward the sink to wash his hands.

"I was hungry," he said simply.

Okay. He wasn't rude or impolite, but he seemed distant just like he had last night. They both got situated at the table with their coffee and plates of food, and after Rose offered a brief prayer, they dug in.

"I guess you got an early start working while I slept in," Rose said, trying to get a conversation going after eating a few bites of her enchilada filled with scrambled eggs and sausage.

Henry looked up at her, and for the first time since he'd walked in, he held her gaze. "You should rest all you can," he said, the slight furrow in his brow softening. "It's the best thing for you. You've been injured."

"It isn't that much of an injury. I imagine in your previous lines of work you were wounded much worse."

Henry shrugged without looking up and kept eating.

Apparently that was something he didn't want to talk about.

"Thank you for risking your life to rescue me last night," she said. *"Again."* Rose really didn't want to sit there and eat in silence. She wanted a conversation. She wanted that connection between them to come back.

"I'd argue that you mostly saved yourself," Henry finally said. "You just needed a little backup. Everybody does at some time."

He looked at her again and Rose really wanted to talk specifically about what was going on between the two of them right now. What had changed? Was he upset with her about something?

At the same time, it didn't seem right to push him for answers. Henry didn't owe her anything. She was the one who owed him a huge debt. He'd helped her stay alive, helped her with her investigation and played a part in her discovery that her parents were in danger and needed help from the cops. Then he'd had his friend Deputy Ruiz initiate a plan to help them. She didn't want to repay Henry by being demanding. Maybe he was just emotional for some reason and didn't care to talk about his feelings. That was his right, even if it was frustrating for her.

"I can't believe you'd ever want to sell this place and move away," Rose said a few moments later, glancing out the kitchen window at the mountain peaks and then focusing her attention on the blackberry vines that Viv had finally succeeded in trimming into a manageable state.

"I don't know for sure what I'll do," Henry said.

When Rose turned back to him, he was taking in the same gorgeous view outside that she had just been enjoying.

"I suppose I could make this a working ranch again," he said thoughtfully. "If Bennie and Viv stayed on to help we could eventually hire on some hands and expand the business in a substantial way."

"It's so beautiful and peaceful up here. I don't know why you'd choose to do anything else," Rose said.

"I've been back in Cedar Lodge for about four months now." Henry rested an elbow on the table. "For a few days at a time I start to feel as if I'm settling in and everything is fine, but the next thing I know I get smacked in the face by some not-so-great memory from my younger days."

That must have been what was bothering him.

"Like what?" Rose asked.

He shrugged. "Family issues, mostly. My parents. When I come across people I haven't seen in a while, they make jokes about how they assumed I'd end up in prison or something along those lines. I know they don't mean any harm and they're just trying to be funny, but it gets tiresome."

"Lots of people aren't born into a perfect family," Rose commented.

"Yeah, well, maybe I'll have a family of my own someday and I wouldn't want my children to have any of those kinds of assumptions placed on them because of how their grandparents behaved. It might be better to just start a new life in a new town."

"I wouldn't put too much weight on other people's opinions," Rose said, while trying to remember whether she'd made any dumb comments that he might have taken to heart. The truth was she had assumed he was still the class clown troublemaker type when he first came to her rescue. And later when he'd talked about his uncertain future, she'd assumed he was still kind of flaky.

She'd been so wrong.

"I bet you thought I was still bossy and argumentative like I was back in high school when you first saw me after so many years had passed," she said in a teasing tone, trying to lighten the mood.

"Yes, I did think that," he said, placing his utensils on his plate and then picking it up as he stood. "And you're still a little bit that way."

"No, I'm not."

He laughed and then she laughed, too, when she realized she'd just inadvertently proven his point.

"I'm not sure what I'm going to do with my life or where I'm going to live," Henry said. "But wherever you end up going and whatever you end up doing, I hope things work out well for you." He walked over to put his dishes into the sink.

Rose remained at the table, feeling a sharp pain like a barb in her heart. His words were polite enough, but they had the feeling of a dismissal. It was the depth of that pain that told her she'd crossed the line and fallen in love with him, whether she'd intended to or not. But it looked as if he didn't feel the same way.

She'd thought he did. She definitely had not imagined the hand-holding and the gentle kisses on her forehead and cheek, or the times he'd taken her up in his arms and offered her his strength when she'd been in desperate need of it.

He had felt the same way as she had or close to it. So why had things changed?

"I'm going to get more work done on the fences," Henry said, grabbing his cowboy hat from the peg on the wall. "I have my phone. Call me if you need anything."

What she *needed* was to know what was happening with him. Or maybe she just needed to accept his decision to create some distance between them. It wasn't fair to place demands on him when she was already staying in his house benefiting from his support, thanks to the fact that he was a decent man who'd made a career of helping to people in dangerous situations.

Perhaps, as was so often the case when she was younger, she just needed to get over herself and her own feelings.

But right now she couldn't do that. That pain in her heart was getting more pointed as she thought of the time in the future when she and Henry would part ways and that would be the end of it.

Her eyes began to burn and she swiped at them before any tears could fall. She was scared for herself and her parents, and apparently she'd lost some of the self-control she'd always been so proud of. But she would pull herself together.

Rose picked up her plate and cutlery and washed her dishes as well as Henry's. It was the least she could do since she was staying in his house and eating his food. She made quick plans to look through the rest of Gabe Kraft's photos and then maybe write down some notes about everything she knew and had experienced and see if she could make any headway figuring things out when it came to Kraft's blackmailing enterprise or anything else for that matter.

She would stay busy while she waited to hear from her parents about how things went with Dylan's sting operation. If Henry could emotionally back away, Rose could stay busy and do that, too.

At least she could fake doing it until her life was no longer in danger. Then she and Henry could get back to their regular lives. Assuming they both survived.

"I'm just happy you didn't blow the operation and lose your chance to capture the guy," Henry teased Dylan at the Bannon County Sheriff's Station.

The deputy rolled his eyes in response before letting go with a quiet laugh.

They were knee-deep in a serious situation trying to keep Rose alive and potentially solve multiple crimes, but as the three of them walked down a hallway at the sheriff's department, Henry couldn't resist making the joke. He was relieved that someone had finally been arrested and now maybe they'd finally make progress on stopping the attacks targeted on Rose.

Henry stole a glance at her walking beside him. Her chin was lifted and the determined set of her jaw told him she was ready to confront the criminal. A warm feeling of admiration for her filled his heart. He knew her well enough now to understand that her ready-to-take-on-the-world demeanor was not simply the combative nature he'd assumed it was.

Rose had her vulnerabilities just like anyone else, and when faced with an obstacle, she did her best to summon up her courage and confront whatever challenge she had to. Now he realized her ability to do that likely came from having to look out for her parents from an early age.

He knew he'd been borderline rude to her this morning at breakfast. He'd seen the startled look on her face as he talked about the finality of going their separate ways as soon as the criminal conspiracy against her was wrapped up. It had hurt him to see her looking like that, as if he'd pulled the emotional rug out from under her feet, which he supposed he had done.

When he thought about it later, it had been tempting to go back to her and apologize, but apologize for what? How could he apologize without changing the message he'd intended to convey and still stood by? They couldn't possibly have a future together when he didn't know what his plans were. He didn't want to get in the way of the plans she already had in place. He didn't want to have a future that was tainted by his family's reputation in the past. Every time he thought he was over it and didn't care what people thought, he would find himself concerned about it again.

Dylan stopped walking and reached for the handle on a closed door. "This is the observation room," he said to

Rose before turning the handle. "You and Henry can watch and listen in from behind a tinted pane of glass while Sergeant Reid and I interrogate the perp. Maybe you'll pick up on some detail that will help with the capture of the other assailants."

"Wait, this creep isn't one of gunmen who've been trying to kidnap or kill Rose?" Henry asked.

"He claims he isn't, but we'll see." Dylan turned back to Rose. "Your parents said they didn't recognize him. But maybe you will."

The small room had dim lighting. There was a wide pane of glass on one wall and a row of padded armchairs in front of it. "Have a seat," Dylan said.

Rose walked ahead of Henry. As soon as she got a good view into the interrogation room, she gasped.

"What?" Henry asked, but then he saw what had triggered her reaction. A familiar-looking man with gelled brown hair sat at a table across from Sergeant Reid.

"Curtis," Rose said in a hushed, shocked voice. "Curtis was threatening to hurt my parents if they didn't pay back their loan? Mom said someone was apprehended but she didn't tell me his name."

"You know this guy?" Dylan asked.

"Curtis Tucker. He lives behind Gabe Kraft's house," Rose said. "He came over and introduced himself to us. Made it sound as if he knew Kraft, but just barely."

Dylan nodded. "Reid and I need to get started. Curtis hasn't lawyered up yet so we're trying to get as much information as we can before he decides to stop talking."

Dylan left and then reappeared in the interrogation room.

Henry listened carefully to the conversation between the cops and Curtis, though much of his attention was drawn to Rose seated close beside him. Did he truly want to walk away from a relationship with her? It seemed like the right thing to do. And yet everything in life seemed so much better when he was with her. Even sitting in this room at the sheriff's station watching Curtis get questioned.

Curtis Tucker was self-assured to the point of arrogance when the questioning began. He displayed a much different persona from the one he had at Kraft's house, where he'd appeared to be a friendly, harmless neighbor. But as Dylan and Sergeant Reid asked more pointed questions—insinuating that Curtis was connected to the violent attacks on Rose—Kraft's former neighbor appeared nervous. He vehemently denied knowing the attackers.

"But they work for you," Dylan said matter-of-factly. "They're the knee-breakers you employ to rough up people who aren't making their loan payments."

"Not true!" Curtis shouted, running his hand through his tufts of gelled hair and completely losing his cool.

"And we know you're involved in blackmail, too."

Curtis admitted that he'd been closer friends with Gabe Kraft than he'd originally let on. He said that Gabe Kraft was proud of his work and liked to brag about it, especially when he was drinking, and he tended to give away some of the specific details.

From the deck at the back of his house, Curtis had watched people come and go at Kraft's house over the last few years. Kraft had a lot of his clients go there to make their payments. Curtis had enjoyed learning who the victims were and Kraft didn't mind telling him about them and gloating over how much money he was making off them.

Curtis admitted he cooked up a simple scheme after Kraft was murdered. He would hide his identity while putting pressure on Kraft's clients to continue making payments. He threatened some of the people to get them to pay, sometimes throwing bricks through home windows or vandalizing cars to increase the pressure. Some of his targeted victims ignored him, but enough of them were frightened and kept the payments going to make it worth the effort. He boasted of making good money, but claimed he was never involved in any physical violence. Eventually he announced that he was finished talking and wanted a lawyer and the interview ended.

"We got a lot more information out of him than I'd expected," Dylan said when he came to collect Henry and Rose. "And we'll likely get more when the criminal charges against him are lined up and he's offered a plea deal to reduce his prison sentence."

"But we learned nothing about the creeps who keep trying to get to Rose," Henry said. "What do you think? Is Curtis really not tied to them or is he a good liar?"

"We'll be working hard to figure that out."

"I'll let my parents know what happened here," Rose said. "Thank you again for your help."

"You're welcome," Dylan said.

Henry had a teasing comment poised on the tip of his tongue for the deputy, but in the end he didn't say it. He was proud of his childhood friend. At moments like this it was worth the rough memories that sometimes accompanied being back in his old hometown. It was good seeing Dylan, Kris and Cole on a regular basis.

Shoving those thoughts aside, he scanned the area as he and Rose walked over to the car she'd insisted on renting after Viv's truck was so badly damaged in last night's attack.

Rose hit the fob to unlock the doors and headed toward the driver's side.

"You sure you don't want me to drive?" Henry asked.

They'd already had this conversation after Bennie had taken them to the car rental office. "I remind you again that I've had training in evasive driving tactics."

She offered him a saucy grin that both thrilled and scared him a little. He really had remained drawn to her despite his best efforts to break that connection.

"We aren't going to need any fancy driving tactics for where we're going next," Rose said after they were inside the car.

"To the repair shop to pick up my truck if they've finished replacing the broken windows and mirror?" Henry asked.

She had her phone out and she was reading something on the screen. "Ah, this is good timing," she said, not having answered his question yet.

"What's going on?"

"I'd wanted to go by Deputy Prosecutor Sloane's office and talk to him about who could have accessed the records of our video call when I was in Utah, among other things," she said before pulling out of the parking lot. "I just saw that Gabe Kraft's murder trial wrapped up early today. It's not five o'clock yet, so maybe Sloane is in his office."

"I'll be interested in hearing what he has to say."

Rose nodded. "Me, too. Also, if we can convince him to take another look at the Boyd Mansion fire and investigate the possibility that it was arson, perhaps we'll get to the bottom of everything and this will all be over."

"Possibly," Henry said. *Or maybe it will have the same effect as hitting a beehive with a stick and make things ten times worse as the guilty parties begin to panic. And that would mean more attacks on Rose.*

No matter what his future plans turned out to be, Henry would remain at her side until he felt certain she was safe.

TWELVE

"My administrative assistant told me you have something important to tell me," Deputy Prosecutor Nate Sloane said to Rose.

"Thank you for taking the time to meet with us," Rose replied, stepping into his office with Henry behind her. "I know you're a busy man."

Sloane gestured at the two visitor chairs in front of his desk. "Please, take a seat."

Rose cleared her throat as soon as she and Henry were settled. "I don't know if you're aware of this, but Gabe Kraft was not only a loan shark. He was a blackmailer, too. I believe the attempts on my life, and possibly even the murder of Kraft, are related to that."

Sloane shook his head. "Gabe Kraft was shot and killed by Lance Preston," he said matter-of-factly. "Preston owed Kraft money, but he couldn't pay. Kraft threatened to hurt Preston or someone in his family if he didn't come up with the money. Preston was angry, got blind drunk, tracked down Kraft and shot him dead. He then passed out at the murder scene where he was found with the murder weapon at hand. The case is as cut-and-dried as it can get."

"I think there was something more going on than that," Rose ventured.

"I don't." Sloane crossed his arms over his chest. "I've put together a solid, straightforward case to convict Lance Preston and shortly after the conclusion of closing arguments tomorrow I expect him to be brought to justice."

"But the blackmail—"

"Doesn't matter," the deputy prosecutor interrupted. "Gabe Kraft is deceased so there's nothing to pursue on that front."

"I believe he was blackmailing Helen Keebler—or someone employed at her estate—about setting the Boyd Mansion fire, causing the death of the poor man who was inside," Rose blurted out, afraid Sloane would dismiss her before she could make her case.

Sloane stilled and stared at her. "You want to accuse Helen Keebler, a very wealthy and powerful woman in this town, of intentionally setting a building that she owned on fire, or arranging for someone to do that? And then you want to tell me that a now-deceased loan shark was blackmailing her?" He shook his head. "Show me your evidence. Show me your proof. Last I heard, there was no legal determination that the fire was caused by arson. It looked as if the transient who'd been staying there had unintentionally started it."

This was not how Rose had anticipated this conversation would go. She'd thought Sloane would be more helpful and consider what she had to say.

Henry reached for Rose's hand.

"The night before I came home from Utah, I told you on our video call that I had seen Kraft driving away from the Keebler estate a couple of times," Rose said, encouraged by Henry's touch.

"I recall that. It's possible he was visiting an employee at the estate, and not Mrs. Keebler."

"I agree," Rose said, struggling to keep the frustration from her voice. "In tracking down two of Kraft's blackmail victims, I spoke to a person who said Kraft bragged that he was blackmailing the person who set the Boyd Mansion on fire."

Sloane continued to stare at Rose, making her nervous. She felt her throat getting dry. This was likely a tactic common to prosecutors and she hoped to never be on the receiving end of it in a courtroom.

"What exactly are you asking me to do?" Sloane finally said.

"Look into this. Open an arson investigation. Find out who passed along the information that I'd seen Kraft coming from the Keebler estate because I believe that is what triggered the attacks on me."

"Someone telling you that the Boyd Mansion fire was arson is not evidence. What facts can you show me?"

"None, actually. But I think if you begin to do a little investigating, you'll soon see that I'm onto something. And maybe, hopefully, you'll find the person pushing for the attacks on me and stop them."

"Let's get back to that video call you had with Rose," Henry interjected. "Who could have seen or heard that or maybe read a transcript of the conversation?"

Rose turned to him, gratitude and affection mingling into a warm sensation in the center of her chest. How had she ever thought him unfocused? He was a very sharp person, probably always had been even back when they were teenagers. He just sorted through information in a way that was different from hers. And she hadn't been able to appreciate that fact until recently.

"Are you suggesting someone on my staff is compromised and they handed off information to criminals?"

Sloane asked calmly, though the expression on his face tightened and his eyes darkened.

Henry responded with a slow shrug. "*Is* someone on your staff untrustworthy? How secure was your live conversation with Rose? Do you track who views a recording of your video calls or reads a transcript?"

The atmosphere in the office felt heated. Rose wasn't sure whether to say something to calm things down or push them to a breaking point. She was frustrated by Sloane's response and sick of getting nowhere in her attempts to understand why she'd been targeted and to get the assailants captured. It was quite possible that the next attempt to kidnap or kill her would succeed. She was tired of being afraid.

She decided to join Henry in calmly waiting out the deputy prosecutor to see how he would respond.

"We maintain strict document security and track all access to everything related to our cases," Sloane finally said, "video calls included. I'll order an audit of who listened to or looked at or read about that call and see if there's anything that appears out of the ordinary. If you're asking me to go beyond that and investigate my trusted employees on your say-so, my response is *no*. Come back with evidence on the topics you've brought to my attention and we'll talk further."

Sloane stood and Rose realized she and Henry had been dismissed.

It was almost closing time and the city administrative building was quiet as Rose and Henry walked down the hallway to the exit.

"I can't believe he just gave me the brush-off and didn't take anything I'd told him seriously," Rose said to Henry.

"I know you're not going to stand for that," Henry replied with a confidence that needled her.

What recourse did he think she had? What could she do?

"My truck is ready to be picked up at the repair shop," he told her, looking at his phone after they'd gotten back into Rose's rental car. "We can get it now or I can have Bennie drive me back to town tomorrow to get it."

That was another thing about Henry that bugged her right now. Why did he have to be so kind and considerate, even taking hold of her hand in Sloane's office, and yet insist on making no lasting connection with her? He'd practically preemptively offered her his final goodbye over breakfast this morning. What was that about?

"Let's go get your truck," she said, not bothering to hide her sullen mood. She was looking forward to getting back to the ranch where hopefully she could figure out the next step in her investigation. Apparently, Henry had already decided there would be no moving forward in their relationship and there wasn't anything she could do about that. She might as well put her mental energy into figuring out how to move forward in her fight to discover the motivation behind the attacks on her while also doing her best to stay alive.

Unfortunately, while she was doing that, she probably wouldn't be able to resist thinking about Henry, too.

"I'll reimburse you for the cost of these repairs," Rose said to Henry at the service counter inside the repair shop. "It's my fault your truck windows were shot out."

It was closing time and the two of them were the only customers inside the cavernous workspace waiting to get their vehicle.

Henry glanced at Rose standing beside him. The expression on her face was so earnest, and for seemingly the millionth time he wished he could bring a quick end to all the threats and violence plaguing her. She was an intelligent, more-than-competent woman, but she didn't have the skills or training necessary to aggressively face the attackers herself.

"I'll pay for the repairs to Viv's truck, too," she added.

"You don't need to pay for any of the repairs," Henry said as the employee at the service counter pulled an invoice off a printer. "I have insurance." He also had money set aside. He'd worked a lot of years with no family to provide for so most of his pay went into savings. Granted, a fair amount was going into the restoration of the ranch right now, but he was still doing fine financially.

Rose opened her mouth to say something, but the growl of an approaching engine outside tugged her attention toward the window behind the service counter.

"People use our property as a shortcut to Elkhorn Avenue all the time," the employee said, hooking a thumb toward the window behind him without turning around. "It would be a little quieter in here if the owner would do something to stop it, but he won't. He says putting up a barrier would be more expense than it's worth."

A black SUV pulled in front of the shop window and stopped. The vehicle's passenger window was down and Henry caught a glimpse of light glinting off something metallic inside. His combat instincts clamored for his attention seconds before the passenger turned toward him and he recognized the face of the blond attacker.

"Get down!" Henry yelled. Using his body as a shield, he pushed Rose toward the ground while fervently hoping the worker behind the counter had gotten out of the way, too.

Bang! Bang! Bang!

The spray of bullets blasted through the glass, one after

another until it seemed as if the shots would never end. Concerned that the thugs would attempt to enter the building, Henry lifted himself away from Rose and then pulled his gun from his waistband. "Stay down and call the police."

"What are you doing?" Rose asked, reaching for the phone in her back pocket.

The shooting had finally stopped, but Henry wasn't sure that was a good thing. He hadn't heard the SUV drive away and if he stood up to look over the counter and out the window, he'd likely get shot. "Wait here," he said, glad to see Rose was already tapping 9-1-1 on her phone. "I'm going to have a look around."

She nodded and then began speaking to the emergency operator.

Henry didn't want to leave her unprotected, and yet he couldn't risk letting the assailants make their way into the repair bay where they could start shooting again. Staying mostly bent over to keep himself from being an easy target for the shooters, Henry lifted up just enough to look and see that the shop window had been completely blown out and the SUV was still idling outside.

"You all right behind the counter?" Henry called out to the employee.

"Yeah." The man's voice came from a different direction, sounding as if he'd crawled to a safer location.

"Anybody hurt?" Henry yelled, directing his voice toward the repair people who'd disappeared behind the vehicles in the work area.

Three or four voices responded that they were all right.

Still crouching, Henry used the counter for cover and moved along the length of it. When he reached the end, he sprinted for the nearby exit door. Easing it open, he anticipated that an attacker would be waiting for him.

With the door open he could hear sirens. The police station was nearby and officers should be here quickly. Normally that would be a good thing. But Henry was tired of the criminals making a clean getaway before the cops could respond. Maybe this time he'd have a chance to take the fight to the assailants before they could flee.

With his muscles tightened in anticipation of whatever action was necessary, Henry pushed the door farther open. Nothing happened, so he stepped out and around the door, moving to press his back against the building so he'd have cover as he peered around the corner. If the SUV was still outside the broken shop window, he'd shoot at the front end of it until there was so much damage that the gunmen couldn't possibly outrun the cops even if the vehicle was still drivable.

An engine roared loudly and the SUV raced past before Henry could follow through on his plan. He managed to fire several shots that struck the vehicle but didn't stop it. The driver sped across the gravel parking area before turning onto a well-worn path through the surrounding grass and weeds that led toward a stand of trees and Elkhorn Avenue on the other side.

Even from this distance Henry could have fired a few rounds at the fleeing vehicle that might do substantial damage. But he couldn't be certain any bullets wouldn't stray beyond the targeted SUV and potentially strike an innocent civilian who walked into the line of fire. Frustrated, he tucked away his gun. He'd noted the license plate number, but the rig was probably stolen.

Back inside the repair shop the workers had come out of hiding. Rose hurried over to Henry, her phone on speaker so he could hear that she was still connected to the emergency dispatch operator.

"They got away," Henry said before she could ask.

"I'm just glad you're okay. I was worried when you went out there."

The counter service employee approached them. "I knew the damage to your windows was done by somebody who'd shot at you on the highway. What's going on? Why are people attacking you?"

Rose let go a laugh with an edge of bitterness. "We don't know. Not for certain, anyway."

The guy shook his head. "That was bizarre. They didn't even try to break in and rob the place, which was what I expected when they started firing."

"Police are on scene," the emergency dispatcher said through Rose's phone as a couple of cop cars pulled up to the building. Two more sped by the blasted-out window, following the path the attackers had taken toward the field and the shortcut to Elkhorn Avenue.

"Thanks," Rose said to the dispatcher, disconnecting as the officers walked inside. She turned to Henry, not saying anything as her eyes began to redden and fill with tears.

Henry had found himself in plenty of dangerous situations in his life because that was the career path he'd chosen. He was trained, usually armed and mentally prepared for whatever he had to face. But Rose had been dragged into the midst of violence through no fault of her own and he could only imagine how hard it was for her to keep going. She'd soldiered on and he respected that. But it appeared now that she was approaching an emotional breaking point, and it tore at Henry's heart to see her like this.

He took her in his arms, disregarding his thoughts about what she might read into it. They would figure out what kind of future personal relationship they might—or might not—have later. Right now he desperately wanted to offer her comfort. And selfishly he wanted the feel of her in his embrace again. To his relief, she didn't push him away. He would have deserved it if she had, after he'd been so cold to her at breakfast. Instead she clung to him and they stood together for a few moments.

As the cops headed over to talk to them, Rose broke away. She stepped back, wiping her eyes and running her hands through her hair before straightening her clothes.

With this brazen attack the assailants had appeared desperate to the point of recklessness and Henry found that unsettling. The attackers had repeatedly escaped capture by the cops, which told him they were likely hired professionals and not just low-life associates of someone with a grudge. By now, whoever had hired them must be putting on the pressure for them to get the job done and grab Rose or silence her forever.

Henry was convinced that Rose witnessing Kraft's visits to the Keebler home was the reason she'd been targeted. And that Thomas Conway's claim that Kraft was blackmailing the person responsible for the Boyd Mansion fire and the resultant death of the squatter also made sense.

Deputy Prosecutor Sloane was blinded by his determination to win a conviction in the murder trial and also by his resentment at the suggestion that one of his employees might have passed along Rose's comments connecting the Keebler family and Gabe Kraft. It was time to go over Sloane's head and talk to his boss, the city attorney.

All Henry knew to do in the meantime was to protect Rose—with his life if he had to, and he was willing to do that. As he headed toward the cops to give them his statement, he glanced at Rose, who had already walked over to speak with them. He realized that he absolutely would protect her as best he could for as long as it took to get everyone involved in these crimes locked up. He also realized that he truly could no longer imagine his life without her. He wished he could be certain that she felt the same way about him. But maybe he had already burned that bridge. If it had ever really existed.

THIRTEEN

"The good news is that we've been able to identify the attackers thanks to images caught by the repair shop security cameras," Kris Volker told Rose and Henry the next morning at the Cedar Lodge Police Department. "The light-haired one is Neil Swift. The man he's been working with is Bruce Moreau."

"I don't suppose it will be as easy as looking up their home address and going there to arrest them," Rose said, trying to keep the cynical tone from her voice and failing. She'd had a rough evening at the ranch following the shooting at the repair shop, and it had become even worse later when she'd learned her mom had suffered her first ever panic attack.

Rose was worried about her mom, and following their phone conversation last night she had tossed and turned without getting much sleep. Even a big mug of coffee this morning hadn't been able to set her to rights. She was exhausted, depressed and afraid to let herself get hopeful that the horrible situation she'd found herself in might finally be resolved. But Kris had called this morning saying he had news, so she was putting in the effort to at least appear optimistic.

"You're right," Kris said to her, "knowing their names doesn't necessarily mean we can locate them right away. But we're doing our best. Both perps are professional hitmen and both are from Portland, Oregon. Cops over there are helping us by searching their residences, talking to known associates and seeing if they can work up a lead on who is employing them here in Cedar Lodge."

Henry reached for Rose's hand but she subtly moved it away. From the corner of her eye she could see his questioning gaze, but she didn't acknowledge it. Maybe he could experience small romantic moments with her despite knowing he'd be walking away soon. That might be how he'd lived while he was in the army and as a private security contractor traveling the globe. But she couldn't do it any longer. Hand-holding might be a small gesture, but for the sake of protecting her heart and the strong emotions his touch stirred up, it had to stop.

"Before I get ahead of myself with what we know regarding the two assailants," Kris continued, "I need you to look at their mug shots for your official confirmation that these are the men who've been attacking you." Kris slid a tablet across the conference room table for Rose and Henry to have a look.

"Yes," Rose affirmed. "This is the creep who was outside Kraft's house on his phone promising to silence me or kill me if he had to," she continued, looking at the image of a blond man with blue eyes. Glaring at the camera, the man wore a familiar expression of contempt. The high-resolution photo almost made it feel as if he were physically in the room and Rose's stomach clenched with yet another round of anxiety.

Kris swiped the tablet screen. "This is Bruce Moreau," he said, gesturing at the image of the second assailant.

"I can confirm that's the second guy," Rose said. "The one I first saw after the explosion at my condo."

"Moreau and Swift have quite a few associates in the criminal world," Kris said. "Portland police might be able to get one of their cronies to turn on them and get us some info."

"Have you gone to look for them at the Keebler estate?" Rose asked.

"If Helen Keebler hired hitmen, she wouldn't let them stay on her property," Henry said quietly. "She wouldn't want to show any connection to them at all. That would be part of the reason why she'd make sure to hire people who weren't from Cedar Lodge or anyplace nearby." He glanced at his old friend. "And barreling out there demanding to come onto the property and search for them would just tip off the criminals that they'd been identified and the cops are onto them, and that would send them further into hiding."

Kris nodded. "Correct. And we also don't want to jump to any conclusions," he added. "At this point there is no evidence connecting the Keeblers or anyone working for them to any crime. The Boyd Mansion fire was deemed accidental, not arson. And Gabe Kraft wasn't exactly an upstanding guy, so it's possible his claim to have witnessed someone setting the fire at the mansion was a complete lie."

"So there's nothing you can do?" Rose asked, her slight hint of optimism already vanishing.

"That's not what I'm saying. The department's goal right now is to capture the perps who've repeatedly attacked you. I've discussed the big-picture situation with Chief Ellis a couple of times, and as long as we don't have any hard evidence connecting Helen Keebler to the mansion fire or even to Gabe Kraft, there's no possible blackmail situation to tie all this conjecture together. For now, we've got an undercover officer observing the Keebler estate and looking for any signs of Swift or Moreau on the off chance that they actually do show up there."

"What can Henry and I do?" Rose asked.

Kris looked at her with concerned expression. "Stay safe. Stay *alive*. Rest at the ranch and let us take care of this."

"Getting some rest might not be such a bad idea," Henry said beside her.

Rose shook her head. "That feels like giving up and I'm not ready to do that." She turned to Henry. "Capturing the attackers isn't enough. If we don't get to the bottom of *why* they were hired, then even if they are put in jail, somebody else will just take their place and continue to come after me."

"Maybe you'll get the answers you're looking for after these two are taken into custody," Henry said.

Maybe. Maybe not. "I should try talking to Sloane again," Rose strategized aloud. "It *had* to be somebody in his office who passed along my comment about seeing Gabe Kraft leaving the Keebler estate. If we could identify that person that might be the information that breaks the case. I'll let him know we're going over his head to his boss if he doesn't cooperate."

"You don't want to press things too hard at Sloane's office right now," Kris said. "Hopefully he hasn't said anything to his employees about your concerns. If there is an informant in his office, we don't want to tip them off that you suspect them."

Rose huffed out a frustrated breath, but also nodded in agreement.

"I realize not taking action is hard for you," Henry said.

"You know me too well." Growing up in an unstable environment, Rose was used to trying to organize or fix things. Trusting someone else to take care of a problem was hard.

"Thank you for all you're doing, Kris," she said, getting to her feet. Henry stood beside her. "I hope it doesn't sound as if I'm unappreciative," Rose added. "I'm very grateful."

"If I'd been through all you've experienced, I'd be edgy, too," Kris assured her. "Does this mean you'll take my advice and go back up to the ranch and try to relax?"

Rose glanced at Henry. "First, I want to go by and see my mom for a few minutes to make sure she's feeling okay. Then we can go back to the ranch."

Henry nodded. "Sounds good to me." He turned to his friend. "Keep us updated."

"I will."

Rose and Henry headed to the exit and into the parking lot, both looking cautiously around even though they were at the police station. Rose noticed Henry starting to reach for her hand and then stopping himself. Her heart ached knowing the connection between the two of them was broken and their personal relationship would likely fade away from here on out. But that was inevitable, wasn't it? So, better to get the pain over with sooner rather than later.

"Don't worry about me. I'll be okay." Rose offered her mother an encouraging smile. "Focus on taking care of yourself."

"I'm not the one anyone needs to be concerned about."

Liz Balfour shook her head. "I just got too worked up thinking about everything that's been happening and my body went haywire and I felt as if I was having a heart attack."

"Don't beat yourself up, honey." Rose's dad wrapped an arm around his wife's shoulder. "We're all worried and scared for Rosie."

The four of them were seated in the living room at her parents' house. Rose's dad had taken time off work to spend the day with his wife following her heath scare. For the moment, both of Rose's parents were working to calm their worried emotions while sharing freshly brewed coffee with Rose and Henry. Liz had removed a pan of orange-cranberry muffins from the oven just after Rose and Henry arrived and the treats were cooling in the kitchen. Despite the emotion of the moment, Rose found the delicious aroma distracting.

"Your mother and I are aware that we got you into this mess," Ricky Balfour said before taking a moment to clear his throat. "If we hadn't taken out that loan from Gabe Kraft five years ago and then told you about it, you would never have met him."

"I'm glad you told me about it," Rose reassured him. Her gaze took in her dad's graying hair and the worry lines on his face, and she was struck by the realization that her parents were getting up there in years and that life hadn't been simple for them. The decisions they'd made—financially and in their unstable work histories—had brought stress into their lives that wasn't easy for them to bear. While the "smarter" decisions they could have made seemed obvious to Rose, they may not have been as apparent to her mom and dad. Wasn't that always the way? The solution to other people's problems seemed so simple to figure out while you were oblivious to your own.

Lord, I'm sorry I've been so judgmental toward my parents.

"If it hadn't been for you setting up that program on our computer for us to track the interest accruing on the amounts we owed and our payments to Gabe Kraft, we would have believed him when he claimed we hadn't completely paid off the debt," Liz said.

Rose had shoved the paper printout at Kraft when he'd shown up at her parents' house. She'd been unafraid in the face of a dangerous criminal because she'd been caught up in knowing that her details were correct. Now that she thought about it, she remembered him smiling in amusement at the time, just before he turned and walked away without any further argument. But her attention to detail had apparently made an impression that resulted in her being dragged into his dangerous and unsavory business affairs after his death.

"What are you going to do now?" Liz asked Rose.

"I'm not sure, Mom." It was just now that Rose realized her parents' mention of their original loan from Kraft was the only time they'd ever directly asked for her help with their finances. It had been Rose's idea to leave college and return to Cedar Lodge when they were facing some of their regular bouts of financial difficulty. In actuality Rose was the one who couldn't stand uncertainty. Her parents might not have enjoyed the financial troubles they'd endured over the years, but they'd adapted to it. Maybe they even had a higher tolerance for it. And that was their right.

Just as it was Henry's right to leave things undecided— like his life plans—for as long as it took for him to find certainty. Rose glanced at him, realizing that if she loosened some of her control-freak tendencies she could enjoy a lot more situations in life without demanding immediate answers or trying to fix things. Her heart squeezed as she thought of Henry emotionally backing away so decidedly at breakfast yesterday morning. In the end, it probably didn't matter what her opinion was on the way he chose to live his life. But she couldn't help thinking about it. Just as she still couldn't help caring for him, or feeling a tremble of excitement in her chest when they accidentally touched or she heard him say her name.

"Well, Rose, you've got to make some kind of decision because Cedar Lodge is obviously no longer a safe place for you." Liz stood from the sofa, taking a deep breath and then brushing the beginnings of tears from the corners of her eyes. "And while you think about that, I'll get the muffins and brew a fresh pot of coffee and be right back."

"We've got family in California," Rose's dad reminded her a few moments later. "Why don't you go down to Santa Cruz and stay with them for a while? You could hang out at the beach."

While listening to her dad, Rose gazed around the room until the expression in Henry's eyes snagged her attention. She perceived an emotion she couldn't quite identify. Sadness, maybe. Or regret. But regret for what? Regret that they hadn't brought an end to the criminal conspiracy that so determinedly targeted Rose? Or regret over something more personal? Like going out of his way to put emotional distance between them at breakfast yesterday morning?

"I haven't been to the beach in ages," Rose responded absently to her dad.

She continued to gaze at Henry for a few more seconds

while feeling a burning combination of tenderheartedness and frustration. Finally she turned away.

For a guy who couldn't seem to shut up when they were in high school, Henry had become pretty closemouthed over the last twenty-four hours. And for a big bad former army ranger and professional hostage negotiator, he seemed ridiculously hesitant to just flat-out tell Rose that he wasn't in love with her and didn't see how he could ever be. Yes, that would be hard for her to hear, but at least it would bring a clear finality to their relationship and her smoldering feelings for him might finally burn out.

"I'm going to go see if Mom needs any help." Rose got to her feet, desperately needing to get away from Henry so she could straighten out her thoughts about him. People were trying to *kill* her, and yet here she was wallowing in sentiments that she felt so sharply she could no longer sit still. She didn't want to look at Henry and wonder what he was thinking. She wanted to pull herself together. She wanted him to pull himself together, too, and admit that he cared for her and they had the beginnings of something special together. That it would be ridiculous to just throw that away, even if they were in the midst of trying to figure out a crime and put an end to the attacks on her.

She *knew* they belonged together. But in this particular situation she was not going to argue her point. She deserved better than that. If Henry couldn't come to the conclusion on his own that he cared for her as much as she cared for him, well, that was that. She would find a way to live with it, though she really didn't want to have to.

Rose shoved open the swinging door into the kitchen, planning to make a beeline to the coffee pot to refill her mug, but there was no freshly made coffee. The muffins were still on a cooling rack rather than a serving platter.

"Mom?" Rose called out. At the far end of the kitchen there was an open doorway leading to a short hallway where a pantry, a laundry room and the door to the backyard were located. Mom had seemed pretty worried for Rose when she'd left the living room. Maybe she'd been overcome with emotion and had stepped outside for a few moments to collect herself.

Rose heard a sound from the pantry area and headed in that direction hoping to comfort and reassure her mother. She rounded the corner and there was her mom, arms clenched across her chest in terror as the dark-haired assailant, Moreau, held the barrel of a pistol pressed to her ear.

Rose's heart stopped.

The blond attacker, Swift, stood in the open doorway to the backyard. And he held a gun pointed directly at Rose. The criminal raised a finger to his lips in a shushing gesture before saying to Rose, "If you call out to your boyfriend, we'll kill your mom."

Rose's jaw dropped. At first the only thing that came out of her mouth was a tight exhale of fear. But then she said quietly, "Let my mom go and we'll step outside. It's me you want." She assumed they'd take their opportunity to end it all right now, and her poor mom didn't need to witness that.

"Our plans are fluid," Swift said quietly. "We're not going to kill you just yet if we don't have to. But we are taking you with us." He nodded at Moreau.

The accomplice moved his gun away from Liz's ear and Rose's lungs eased slightly. But then Moreau struck Liz on the side of the head with his fist and she slumped to the floor.

"Mom!" Rose called out, lunging toward her mother.

Swift intercepted her before she could reach Liz, clamping his hand across Rose's mouth. The men forced Rose out of the house while she fought unsuccessfully to look back at Liz. *Lord! Please let my mother be okay!*

The creeps shoved Rose and forced her to keep moving toward the forest at the edge of the property. "Where are you taking me?" she demanded, barely able to catch her breath.

"Don't worry so much," Swift told her, his gun pressed against the back of her head. "It will all be over soon."

FOURTEEN

When Rose disappeared into the kitchen to help her mom, a little bit of Henry's heart went with her. Which was ridiculous and not at all like him to think that way. But it was indeed how he felt. Probably because there had just been talk of Rose leaving town, and the possibility of that happening had made him realize that he really had fallen in love with her.

Going their separate ways? Nope, not something Henry wanted anymore. Living his life without her and returning to his existence as a guy with plenty of friends but no special woman in his life was not at all appealing. He would not give up on the possibility of a future with her. Henry was a fighter, and he'd fight through whatever he had to so he could make this relationship work. He took comfort in knowing that Rose was a fighter, too.

Crash!

Something metallic had hit the floor in the kitchen.

"Liz? You girls all right in there?" Ricky called out.

When there was no immediate reply, Henry shot to his feet and rushed to the kitchen. He shoved open the swinging door and saw neither Rose nor her mother. A weak groan from the floor on the other side of the kitchen island caught his attention. He rushed around to find Liz collapsed on the ground with a metallic mixing bowl and wooden spoon beside her. It appeared she'd knocked them off the counter while trying to grab hold for balance.

"What happened?" Henry squatted beside her, noting a red lump on the side of her face that was already beginning to swell.

Moaning, Liz began to sit up.

"Call 9-1-1!" Henry yelled loud enough for her husband to hear in the living room and then he turned back to her.

"They've got Rosie," Mrs. Balfour said weakly, her eyelids fluttering. "Two men. They went out the back door with her."

Ricky hurried into the kitchen, already tapping his phone.

"I'm going to get Rose!" Henry took off running, leaving Mr. Balfour to arrange for an ambulance.

By the time Henry hit the back door, he'd already drawn his gun from his waistband.

He didn't immediately spot anything out of the ordinary. Like all the other properties on this side of the street, the backyard had no fence but instead offered an unblocked view of thick forest. The two men could have taken Rose in that direction, or they could have taken her to a vehicle parked on the street and then driven her away.

Henry raced through the side yard to the front of the house, but he didn't see or hear a getaway car speeding off in the distance. The neighborhood was quiet.

Heart hammering in his chest, Henry returned to the backyard and began scanning the ground for any hint of a trail left behind by Rose and the criminals who'd taken her. The lawn appeared recently mowed and the short blades of grass didn't give away any clues. Henry shifted his attention to the edge of the property, studying the mixture of dirt and fallen pine needles until he spotted a section that appeared recently disturbed.

He pushed aside the pine tree branches and headed into the woods. The forest grew thicker the farther Henry went, and it became easier to spot broken twigs and branches that told him which direction to go.

The ground sloped downward. Rose's parents lived on a hillside and the attackers were headed downhill, which made sense. At the bottom was the two-lane highway and a collection of small businesses with a paved parking lot where the criminals had likely left their vehicle.

Henry grabbed his phone and tapped 9-1-1.

As soon as dispatch answered, he told them who he was and what was happening. "I'm approaching Cider Cross-roads from the north," he said, continuing to talk over the dispatcher's routine questions because he didn't have time for that and he needed to catch up with the criminals as quickly as possible. "It looks like the perps are headed in that direction. I'll make my presence known to respond-ing officers as soon as they arrive and meet up with them there." Then he disconnected.

He shoved his phone into his pocket and shifted from a jogging pace into a full-out run now that he knew where they were going. The attackers had shown from the begin-ning that they were willing to end Rose's life if they felt they had to. Henry was grateful that he still had an oppor-tunity to recover her alive. He just needed to catch up with them before they shoved Rose into a vehicle and vanished with no way for Henry to ever find them.

Rose did her best to drag her feet, stumble, fall and do everything else she could think of to make it harder for the men who'd captured her to take her to whatever final destination they'd planned.

"Enough!" Moreau barked, grabbing a handful of Rose's hair and yanking her to her feet after she'd let herself fall to her knees again.

Rose yelped in pain, but her cry was muffled by the bandanna tied across her mouth. Her hands were tied behind her back as well, which would make it difficult to run if she managed to somehow get free.

The forest began to thin. Ahead, between the towering pines, she caught glimpses of buildings. Cider Crossroads Country Store, of course. She'd been disoriented after getting kidnapped but now she had her bearings.

At the edge of the clearing, the kidnappers brought Rose to an abrupt halt. The back of Cider Crossroads Country Store was visible directly in front of them. Beside it was the diner and then a crafts supply shop, followed by a couple of other small businesses. Rose couldn't see the parking lot in front, but there were vehicles parked in the back—possibly employees—including a green SUV parked in a more isolated section of the lot.

"Just a few more yards and we're home free," Swift said to Moreau, and Rose watched his gaze settle on the SUV. "But you never know who's looking and might try to stop us," Swift added with a glance at his partner. He tucked his gun into the waistband of his jeans and pulled his shirt hem down to cover it.

Moreau did the same thing with his weapon. "If you try to run or scream, it will be the last thing you do," he said to Rose as he untied her hands and then took the bandanna from her mouth.

Maybe it's worth the risk. Was she really going to let them take her away from any hope of getting help and then do whatever they intended to do? No. But if she started running would they shoot her in the back? Probably. *Lord, please help me.*

"We're just going to walk calmly to that SUV over there," Moreau said, putting his hand on Rose's shoulder and giving her a push.

She'd only taken a couple of steps and barely made it onto the asphalt when she heard a sound like a rockslide behind her. The two hitmen turned just as she did.

"Henry!" she cried out.

The tree branches and forest shadows kept her from getting a clear view, but she knew it was him. And he was racing down the hillside, dislodging rocks and dirt along the way.

"Stop! Let her go!" Henry commanded.

Each of the men grabbed one of Rose's arms and rushed her forward, but Henry was gaining on them. "Stop or I'll shoot!" Henry called out, prompting the assailants to drag her forward even faster. Then, finally, he shouted, "Rose! Get down!"

She dropped her head and bent her knees, which brought her closer to the ground.

Bang!

The bullet went wide and struck a section of pavement away from the buildings. Rose was certain Henry had done that on purpose, intending to intimidate the attackers without risking real harm to Rose. She turned her head and saw that Henry had moved to block the kidnappers' access to their SUV, prompting them to change direction and pull Rose toward the nearby back door of the country store.

Swift grabbed the door handle and turned it, but it was locked. He let go of Rose to pull off his hoodie, wrap it around his fist and then punch the glass window of the old building, quickly clearing a space to reach in, unlock the door and then open it. He hurried inside the store and Moreau shoved Rose in behind Swift before following and slamming the door shut. He engaged the lock and then shoved a supply cabinet in front of the door as a makeshift barricade. It wouldn't be enough to keep Henry out if he was determined to get inside, but it would slow him down.

Ahead, Swift was already screaming threats at whoever was in the store, promising to kill them on the spot of they didn't cooperate. The plan for a stealthy getaway had obviously gone off the rails and now both assailants were edging toward panic with their guns drawn.

Roughly a third of the store space was taken up by bistro tables and chairs in front of a coffee counter with an espresso machine and baked goods. Swift waved his gun around and ordered everyone in the store to move to that area. The two female employees gathered together with an older couple, a man probably in his thirties and a woman with two young girls, all of them wide-eyed and terrified.

"Cover them!" Swift shouted to his partner while the blond assailant ran to the front door to lock it and pull down the shade.

The back door rattled and Swift raced over to fire several shots in that direction. Fear reached up into Rose's throat, and she sent up a frantic prayer while trying to swallow the lump of near panic that threatened to choke her. *Please, Lord, protect Henry.* She had no doubt he was the person trying to get inside and help everyone who was in danger.

"Swift! Moreau! Come out and we can talk." Henry's voice sounded strong and calm from the direction of the back door despite having just been shot at.

"If you only want me, why not let everyone else go?" Rose demanded, not wanting anyone else to get hurt.

"Because right now they're my insurance. Almost like bodyguards, in a way."

Fear mingled with disgust. "You'd hide behind children?" Rose said in a low voice, glancing at the little girls.

Swift offered her a chilling smile. "Of course."

With that, he took a few steps to look toward the barricaded back door. "Stay away!" he shouted at Henry. "If you come through this door, I promise I'll shoot somebody and their blood will be on your hands."

"Police are on their way," Henry hollered back. "Once they get here, it's all over for you. Why don't you forget about your hostages and just go? I saw you running toward the SUV out here. That yours? I'll stand back and let you get in it and drive away as long as you don't take anybody with you."

"Hurry up and think of something," Moreau prodded his partner. "The cops will be here soon. We've got to get out of here."

Swift took a few steps back and looked at the hostages. Keeping his gun pointed toward them, he strode to the front of the store and took a quick look at the customer parking lot. "Everybody take out your key or key fob." Swift barked out the words as he spun around. He strode back to the short hallway where he could keep an eye on the back door and Henry.

With his voice carrying through the broken back door window despite the cabinet that had been placed there, Rose could hear Henry continuing to offer the criminals safe passage to their getaway vehicle if they let the hostages go free.

Swift grabbed a bistro table and pulled it over to a spot where he could keep an eye on the hostages and the back door at the same time. "Put your keys or fobs right here."

Moreau kept a close eye on Rose as the hostages pulled out their fobs to set them on the table.

Swift picked up one of the fobs. "This for the blue truck outside?"

When no one answered right away, he stalked toward the hostages. The woman with the two young girls wrapped her arms tighter around their shoulders before saying, "Yes. That's for our truck."

Swift shoved the fob into his pocket and strode toward the back door. "We don't want to go to prison for murder," he hollered out to Henry. "We're just hired guns and we're not getting paid enough to get locked up for the rest of our lives. Allow us safe passage to our SUV and we'll let the hostages go free. We're hanging on to Rose to guarantee you won't shoot us or try to follow us. As soon as we're away and in the clear, we'll let her go, too. Promise."

"Free everyone and you can go!" Henry hollered back.

"Not a chance! But we'll let some hostages go in a few minutes as a sign of good faith."

"What exactly is the plan?" Moreau asked his accomplice nervously.

"Make Mr. Heroic out there think we'll be heading out the back for our SUV." He stopped at that point to hit the button on a fob that would apparently start the SUV's engine. "He'll believe we're coming out the back door while you and I and his girlfriend will be heading out the front where we'll drive away in our nice new blue truck."

Rose's stomach turned to ice. She'd hoped that Henry would somehow free her from here. She was getting out of the store, all right, but as a hostage to the kidnappers. She gazed at the woman with the two young daughters, and then at the store employees and other patrons. At least these innocent people would be set free.

The only thing Rose could do was try to stay alive until an opportunity to escape presented itself. Or maybe that wasn't going to happen. Maybe this was just the end for her.

"What's going on?" Henry yelled.

"Make way," Swift hollered back. "I'm going to shove the supply cabinet away from the door and then everybody's coming out." He turned to his criminal partner and said, "Grab her," with a nod toward Rose.

Moreau grabbed Rose's upper arm while Swift barked at the hostages, "Everybody get up and get moving. *Now!*"

The hostages streamed out the back door, while Swift and Moreau literally dragged Rose to the front after she refused to cooperate and walk with them. Swift unlocked the door, hit a button on the fob to unlock the blue truck and yanked on Rose's arm. He leaned toward her face. "Start walking or I'll knock you out cold."

Rose started walking.

They got into the truck, with Rose hurriedly shoved into the back seat of the double cab before Swift hit the gas to peel out of the parking lot while the wail of an approaching siren grew louder.

The kidnappers sped onto the road just as a police car raced up, striking its front bumper against the side of the truck and causing it to swerve.

The criminals cursed while Rose gripped her seat as tightly as she could and sent up silent prayers for protection. She didn't want to get into a crash, but she would take that over whatever the kidnappers and their employer had in mind for her.

Bump.

The cop car hit them again, this time sending them spinning toward the forest on the side of the road. In an instant, they crashed into a tree and came to a sudden stop, airbags deploying in front of the criminals and at the side in the back where Rose was seated.

The sudden jolt of it all was shocking. For a moment Rose wasn't sure if she was injured, if the truck was still moving, or exactly what was happening. She shoved away the side airbag and her gaze fell on the door handle. In the next instant she grabbed it and pulled on it and thankfully the door opened.

"Stay there!" Moreau tried to yell at her, but his voice was muffled by the deflating airbag in front of him and she was fairly certain he couldn't see her clearly enough to shoot her. This was likely her only chance at escape and she took it.

Stumbling away from the truck, her head ached and she felt dizzy. Her attempt to run had her staggering without covering much forward distance. *Don't fall,* she commanded herself. Focused only on the ground in front of her and her next steps, she heard the attackers getting out of the truck and shouting at her.

She looked up and saw the cop car that had pushed the truck off the road. Kris Volker exited the squad car, gun drawn, ordering the kidnappers to get face down on the ground. Rose kept moving, not sure if the attackers were still chasing her or if they'd obeyed Kris's command. Fear propelled her, along with the haunting, grinding feeling that she would never be safe.

A sound on the road ahead caught her attention and she spotted a small sedan she didn't recognize. It pulled up toward her and her heart sank. Had she thought she was finally free only to be captured again?

But as the car slowed she realized the driver was one of the employees who'd been held hostage at the store. She also recognized the passenger who shoved open his door before the car even stopped and got out to rush toward her.

"Henry." Rose wobbled on her feet as she came to a stop, overwhelmed with relief to know he was okay. And that he was here, with her.

Henry threw an arm around her, pulling her close to him, while he drew his gun with the other hand and kept it pointed at the kidnappers so that together with Kris they had the two assailants under complete control.

Approaching sirens screamed as police and deputy sheriffs pulled up to assist. Rose counted six vehicles. Within moments Henry must have decided the scene was secure enough, because he tucked away his gun and turned to Rose, his eyes dark with emotion.

"Are you all right?" he asked gently.

"I will be." Her head and neck hurt, and her body still felt as if an electrical surge of adrenaline flowed through it after all she'd just been through, including the crash. But then Henry wrapped both his arms around her and pulled her close. His warmth flooded through her body, bringing with it the comfort she couldn't have imagined a moment ago.

"I was so afraid I'd lost you," Henry said, his words seeming to rumble through his chest as he held Rose close. "I had so many things I was concerned about when I returned to Cedar Lodge after being away for so long, but when I realized those criminals had snuck away from the store and they had you with them, I knew none of those other worries mattered at all."

He took a deep breath, then relaxed his hold on Rose without letting go of her.

"When it looked as if my life might be about to end, I realized there were a lot of things I was worried about that really didn't matter, too," Rose said. She moved her head back just enough to see his face and look into his eyes, hoping to see her own emotions mirrored there. Most especially love. Love for Henry Walsh filled her heart with tenderness and courage. He made her life better. He made her minutes and hours better when they were together.

Rose squared her shoulders, ready to make her argument and convince him they were good together and he should give the two of them a chance. But before she could, Henry placed his hands on either side of her face and then leaned down to gently press his warm lips against hers.

Rose instantly forgot what she was about to say, as her pulse sped up and her chest felt as if it filled with celebration sparklers. Henry's kiss lingered as he moved his hands to the small of her back and he held her closer. When the kiss ended, Rose had the alarming sensation that if he let go of her, she would float away because she didn't feel at all like the same woman she had been before that kiss.

She felt like a woman who belonged with Henry Walsh. And that Henry belonged with her. Maybe this connection had started when they were back in high school and they were both too stubborn to realize it. But now, thirteen years later, they were too stubborn to let it slip away.

Rose was anxious to get back to her parents' house so she could check on her mom. Meanwhile, maybe the arrest of the two gunmen would finally lead to the discovery of who exactly was behind all the attacks. And maybe Rose and Henry could finally be together without having to worry about someone trying to kill them.

FIFTEEN

Henry looked around at his three childhood buddies who were relaxing on the chairs and sofas in the living room of his ranch house. Then he turned to lean over and kiss Rose, who was seated beside him.

"Look at you, Romeo," Dylan teased.

Attackers Swift and Moreno had been arrested yesterday afternoon following their hostage event at the country store. Since then, progress in the criminal case had happened in uneven leaps and all the details had not been reported publicly. While Kris and Dylan knew some of the facts due to their line of work, they didn't know the most recent updates. And Cole was out of the loop almost completely.

"So the deal is, I get you caught up on everything about the crime and you help me finish my fence project," Henry teased his friends. Winter would hit before anyone knew it and Henry needed that task completed before then. Besides, since it looked as if he was back in Cedar Lodge to stay, there was no reason not to take advantage of his friends' generosity and ranch maintenance skills. Because that's what buddies were for.

After a little more joking, all three friends officially agreed to the deal.

Viv and Bennie were in the living room, too, having

made deli-style sandwiches for lunch for everybody. They'd also handed out dishes of homemade blackberry cobbler with ice cream.

Henry looked again at Rose, and when she smiled, his heart felt in danger of overexpanding in his chest. He leaned down for another quick kiss that actually ended up lingering for a few moments, before he straightened up and focused on his friends.

"Let's go already," Cole said in a teasing tone. "I've got a wife and a grandpa and a bunch of other people waiting for me to message them with the details as soon as I get the inside scoop."

"Keep your shirt on," Henry said. "Rose has a presentation to share since it's clearly her story to tell."

"Wait," Cole interrupted, "is this going to be like back in high school when Student Council President Rose Balfour gave her slideshow presentations complete with spreadsheets?" He turned to Rose. "I remember you droning on about boring things like returns on investment at the student store when all any of us cared about was whether we'd be able to buy our favorite candy."

Rose laughed, something she'd done a lot since they'd received word from Police Chief Ellis that the criminal conspiracy had been wrapped up and Rose no longer had anything to worry about.

"I think this presentation will be a lot more interesting, so everybody listen up and take notes," Rose said tartly.

"That's my girl." Henry broke into a wide smile.

Rose tapped the screen of a tablet in her lap and directed a frozen video image of a Cedar Lodge police cruiser onto the flatscreen on the wall. Then she hit the Play arrow and the camera angle moved back to show two officers leading a woman dressed in a chic red designer suit to the cop car and then placing her in the back seat. Her handcuffs glinted in the bright sunlight. The camera then pulled back to offer a view of the stately home the woman had just exited before panning to show the deep blue waters of Bear Lake on the edge of the Keebler estate property.

"Everybody in town already knows that Helen Keebler was arrested and charged with arson and murder last night," Dylan commented as a local news anchor spoke over the video images giving an accounting of the arrest.

"It's odd to see Helen Keebler like that," Viv remarked from her seat on a hassock in front of the screen. "Looking so elegant while getting arrested. Almost regal, actually. A good reminder that appearances can be deceiving."

"She might have thought of herself as royalty," Rose said as the video ended and she queued up another one.

"Who's this guy?" Bennie asked as another image of someone being arrested appeared. This time, it was a man with reddish hair.

"He was just arrested a couple of hours ago," Rose said.

"Deputy Prosecutor Nate Sloane," Dylan muttered. "Man, I did not see that one coming."

The news reporter's voice-over for this segment was brief, with the journalist commenting that specific charges were pending. Then he moved on to a related story. Lance Preston, the man Sloane had been prosecuting for the murder of Gabe Kraft, had been released from custody and all charges against him had been dropped. "This is a continuing story," the newscaster said. "Follow us online or through our social media accounts to stay updated."

"All right, enough with the information that's already public knowledge," Kris said, sitting up straighter on the sofa. "I'm trying to enjoy my scheduled day off after pulling you guys out of the fire yesterday. And being that I'm off rotation, I am currently out of the loop on all the details that haven't been related to the press yet. I'm here to help with the fencing, but I want the facts I was promised."

"Yes, sir," Rose said with a grin before casting an image of the Keebler estate driveway to the flat-screen TV on the wall. "Let me start at the beginning. My friend lives near the spot where this photo was taken. And around this point is where I saw Gabe Kraft leaving the Keebler estate on a couple of different occasions. Casually mentioning that to Nate Sloane on a video call is what nearly got me killed."

"The deputy prosecutor was on the Keeblers' payroll?" Dylan asked.

Rose nodded. "He's Helen Keebler's nephew."

"What does that have to do with anything?" Bennie asked, obviously confused.

Rose took a deep breath and Henry wrapped an arm around her shoulder. He knew from experience that recounting traumatic events could be cathartic, but they could also be triggering. And he'd already reminded her that if talking about everything got to be too much, she could stop at any time. His curious friends and relatives could wait to get the information from public sources like everybody else.

"Everything started with Helen Keebler having expensive tastes along with a gambling habit made worse by frequent trips down to Las Vegas," Rose said. She glanced at her tablet and then set it aside, turning her attention to her friends instead.

"Helen had gone through all the family money that she had personal access to. Much of the Keebler family wealth is in trusts and businesses and set up in ways that no single member can just take it."

"So she really needed to sell that property to the developer because she truly needed the money," Kris said, obviously trying to put together some of the pieces to the puzzle. "I assume she owned that specific piece of property outright and that she had someone set the Boyd Mansion on fire to get the conservationists out of the way so she could sell it to the developer and get her money."

"Surprisingly, Helen set the fire herself, with help from Swift and Moreau," Rose said. "And Gabe Kraft got pictures of her doing it."

"Wait a minute," Dylan interjected. "How did Kraft happen to be there when she started the fire?"

"Gabe Kraft had a friend who was employed as a housekeeper at the estate. The friend overheard Helen talking about the arson plan with someone, possibly her nephew Sloane, and this friend told Kraft about what she'd learned. After that, Kraft made a point of tracking the nighttime activities at the estate until he caught Helen leaving at about one o'clock in the morning. He captured all of the images he needed when she set the mansion ablaze."

"Did any of the pictures you brought back here from Kraft's house show her setting the fire?" Viv asked.

Rose shook her head. "Turns out Kraft had reason to be wary of technology. Last night, detectives visited the homes of Kraft's relatives and went through the stuff they'd taken from his house. They found a couple of digital cameras. The data cards with images of Helen Keebler at the fire were still in them. The relatives had no idea."

"So I'm going to guess that Kraft threatened Helen Keebler with exposing her and she had him murdered," Kris said. "Probably by those two creeps Swift and Moreau. And then she and Sloane framed one of Kraft's known loan-sharking victims, Lance Preston, to go to prison for the murder of Kraft. At that point everything was nicely tied up. Keebler sold her property to the developer and got her money, the blackmailer Kraft was dead, some innocent person was blamed for the murder and that was the end of it."

"That's most of it," Rose agreed. "Everyone in town was astonished when it became public knowledge that Kraft had left me his house in his will. I know I was shocked. And then, just as the trial was about to start, Sloane learned that I had seen Kraft leaving the Keebler estate more than once. Presumably, Kraft was going out there to collect his blackmail payments.

"Keebler and Sloane both assumed that I knew Kraft better than I actually did, and that he'd shared information with me or left me evidence that would send them both to prison. In a way, they were right. I think he wanted me to organize whatever information I could find at his home as best I could and then figure out who killed him if he did indeed get murdered by one of his victims someday. A gamble on his part that paid off.

"Swift and Moreau have gotten a plea deal and they're giving up lots of information," Rose continued. "They're saying that at first Helen just wanted her hired criminals to prevent me from giving testimony in court and potentially divulging information that would be a problem for her." Rose's voice caught in her throat and she stopped to take a breath and wipe at her eyes. Henry tightened his arm around her and she rested her head on his shoulder. "Then she changed her mind. She wanted me taken alive, if possible, so she could discover what specific information I had about her and who I might have shared it with. After that, she planned to have me killed."

Henry already knew all of this information, but the reminder that he could have lost Rose forever still rattled him. He couldn't imagine his future without her, and he didn't want to try.

"That's quite a story," Cole said. "I am grateful to God that you made it through everything."

"Amen," Henry whispered in Rose's ear before placing a lingering kiss on her forehead and then another one on her temple.

"Also, let me add that was a very interesting presentation you just gave, Rose," Cole said with a smile, lightening the mood a little. "Not boring at all. You've come a long way since your time on student council."

"Have you got anything else for us?" Kris asked, getting to his feet. "Otherwise, I want to get to work on that fence so I can get back to my family."

Rose shook her head. "That's it."

Everybody got to their feet.

"I want to thank you again for helping my parents and for capturing Curtis Tucker," Rose said to Dylan.

The deputy shrugged off her words of appreciation, quietly saying that he'd just done his job.

All three of Henry's old school friends had grown up to be extraordinary men who'd come back to their hometown after years away in service to their country. And now they went above and beyond to help their fellow citizens of Cedar Lodge every day.

Henry could hardly believe he'd ever been foolish enough to consider leaving Cedar Lodge again after coming back home and reconnecting with everybody. Whatever challenges popped up if he stayed here, he'd face them head-on.

Bennie and Viv went into the kitchen to put away the leftover cobbler and then give the dogs and Melvin the cat a snack. Henry's friends moved to the front door to get to work. Henry would join them in a few minutes, but right now his arm was wrapped around Rose and he didn't want to let go. It felt so right having her beside him. And he got the impression she felt the same way.

Finally the two of them walked outside.

"I'm going to need to head back to my condo tonight and go back to work in a day or two," Rose said, moving from Henry's embrace to lean her back against a nearby section of fence and look up at him. "I'm going to miss being out here at the ranch every day."

Henry understood why she would need to move back to her own home, but that didn't mean she had to stay away from the ranch. "Quit your job and come work for me, here." He wouldn't say he felt panic at the thought of going long stretches of time without seeing her, but the desperate sense of unease at the thought of them being apart was quite unpleasant.

Rose looked at him with a warm gaze that nearly made his heart stop. "I appreciate that offer, but you can't afford to hire me."

"Sure I can. I have money saved up. I can use that."

"No." She shook her head. Then she pushed away from the fence to gesture toward the stables and the barn. "You have all these expenses and no money coming in. That's no way to run a business. Besides, you might decide to move away."

Henry stared at her for a moment. "Rose," he began patiently, "I'm not going to move away. I'm here for good. And this was supposed to be a romantic moment. Do you have to be so practical right now?"

"I do." She nodded hard enough to make her hair bounce. "I love you and I don't want to see you waste your money or end up losing your ranch to creditors." She stopped talking and looked away with reddened cheeks as if suddenly realizing what she'd just said.

"You *love* me, Rose Balfour?" Henry said, delighted to discover that a hint of the old Henry Walsh teasing tone still lurked within him. He stepped closer and Rose retreated until her back was pressing against the fence again.

Henry moved as close as he dared, breathing in the lavender scent of Rose's shampoo and feeling her exhalations as they moved lightly across the base of his neck.

"Ah…" Rose looked everywhere but at Henry while her cheeks turned even redder.

Henry took both of her hands, brushing his lips across each one and then sliding his own hands up her arms until he was embracing her again. Pressed together, he could feel her heart beating as rapidly as his. It made sense that their heart rates would beat the same, because beneath all their surface differences they were clearly a match.

He leaned back a little, and while he meant to say something witty he ended up just kissing her instead. The sweet sensation of her lips pressed to his almost made him lose his train of thought, but not quite.

"I love you, Rose Balfour," he murmured after their kiss ended. "If you want to leave town and go to college someplace, I'll go with you. But I'm not concerned about being unhappy if I stay in Cedar Lodge anymore. I don't care what people think or what they remember about me or my parents back in the old days. My life started over again when I came back to town and met up with you."

Rose's eyes filled with tears as a smile crossed her lips. "I'm ready to let go of some old plans and worries myself. Maybe we should scrap everything we thought we wanted to do separately and make a new plan for the future together."

"Exactly what I was thinking," Henry said, and then he leaned in for another kiss.

ONE YEAR LATER

"Thank you, Mrs. Walsh. It's always a pleasure doing business with you."

Mrs. Walsh.

Rose and Henry had been married for two months, but Rose was still getting used to that fact. The reminders of her new situation in life resulted in tiny jolts of delighted surprise throughout her day. This was real. She and Henry Walsh had reconnected after thirteen years apart and they'd finally figured out that the edgy tension between them was actually attraction. And after that they'd gotten *married*.

Jimmy, the tech troubleshooter that Rose had worked with at her old job in the insurance office, offered her a smile after she tapped her phone screen and sent him payment for the installation work he'd just completed. He said something else, but Rose wasn't really listening. She was anxious for him to be on his way so she could go kiss her husband.

Determined to be polite despite her feelings, Rose stood and chatted with Jimmy for a few more minutes, glancing out the window behind him every now and then to enjoy the beautiful view of the ranch and towering mountains behind it. That scene never got old.

Finally Jimmy was ready to leave and Rose walked him to the door of her office. It was in a building near the ranch house with several other offices plus a large conference room to allow adequate space for their new business venture, United Protection Services. While Bennie and Viv would manage the ranch, Henry would run a business teaching gun safety, self-defense skills, wilderness survival training and a whole lot more. Henry's old friends would be among that staff, contributing their knowledge on a part-time basis. Rose got to oversee and manage it all—the ranch and the protection services business—and she loved it.

She loved her life with Henry.

She *loved* Henry.

She spotted him outside and her heart melted like butter. Kris, Cole and Dylan had arrived along with their wives and Kris's young son. Rose watched her black-haired cowboy *husband* walk up to the six-year-old boy and then lead him to a horse at the nearby corral railing, where the two of them gave the chestnut mare several nice pats and scratches on the neck.

That was something she'd learned about Henry Walsh over the last year. He was great with kids. Rose hoped they'd have one of their own soon. She started walking toward the group that had moved toward the front steps of the house. Viv and Bennie had cooked a big dinner of smoked beef brisket with a ridiculous number of side dishes and everybody was here to celebrate United Protection Services' first group of students who would be showing up for classes next week.

The attacks on Rose and Henry and the entire shady conspiracy with Gabe Kraft and Helen Keebler and the arson fire at the Boyd Mansion felt like it had happened a very long time ago, even though it had only been one year. The attackers Swift and Moreau had traded information and testimony for lighter sentences, but they were still going to prison for their crimes—including the murder of Gabe Kraft. Helen Keebler would also be spending time behind bars for setting the fire that killed the homeless man inside the mansion, and her nephew, former Deputy Prosecutor Sloane, was facing several serious charges, most of them having to do with misusing the power of his former office.

Rose's parents were doing well. Rose had sold her condo and the house she inherited from Gabe Kraft and while most of that money had gone into the new businesses, she'd set a little aside so she could help her parents if they got into a financial jam again, though she didn't tell them about that. They seemed to be trying to change their ways and become more financially responsible, but only time would tell how that would turn out. And Rose had Henry to help her make wise decisions when it came to that situation.

"Hey," Rose said to Henry, sidling up beside him and feeling that little bit of happy fluttering in her heart that appeared every time she saw him.

"Hey," Henry said in return, his low voice sending the fluttering sensation to the pit of her stomach. He turned and leaned down for a kiss, wrapping his arms around Rose and pulling her close, the scent of leather and pine tree and horses pushing her happiness nearly to the point of making her lightheaded.

"There's the happy couple," Dylan teased them.

Rose felt her face redden as she and Henry reluctantly ended their kiss.

"I'm still amazed you two ended up together," Cole said with a hint of wonder in his voice.

"Me, too," Kris added. "Just goes to show you God really does have a plan for everybody."

Viv appeared at the front door calling everyone to come inside and start eating before the food got cold. Rose and Henry stepped back to allow their guests to go in and begin attacking the delicious food first. Once the crowd moved through, it was just the two of them left on the porch. Plus, Melvin the cat, who was taking a bath at his usual post on the porch railing.

"I love you," Henry said before leaning down to Rose for yet another kiss.

"I love you, too." Rose never got tired of hearing the words or saying them.

Her cowboy husband turned and looked at the new buildings on the property and the new horses in the corral and then glanced back at the house toward the sound of their friends inside bursting into laughter over something obviously entertaining.

"This is going to be fun," he said with a grin. "Our lives, the businesses, living here at the ranch, all of it."

Rose grinned in response because there was no way she could resist. Right now she felt happiness all the way down to her toes.

"It already is fun," Rose said before giving him a playful shove toward the door. "Let's get in there and start enjoying the celebration."

She hoped that every day for the rest of their lives she and Henry would remember to appreciate and celebrate the blessings God had given them. Most especially, the blessing of bringing them back together.

* * * * *

If you liked this story from Jenna Night,
check out her previous Love Inspired Suspense books:

Unsolved Montana Investigation
Witness Protection Ambush
Deadly Ranch Hideout

Available now from Love Inspired!
Find more great reads at www.LoveInspired.com.

Dear Reader,

We never know how things will turn out in our lives, do we?

Facing an uncertain future can be unsettling. But it can also be exciting and fun when blessings we never anticipated come our way as they did with Rose and Henry.

God truly does have a plan for everyone and we can take comfort in that.

Thank you for hanging out with me in Cedar Lodge, Montana, and for reading this story about a couple brought back together under some pretty tough circumstances. So glad they made it through okay! Also glad they found it in their hearts to offer each other a bit of forgiveness and grace. We could all use that.

I invite you to visit my website, JennaNight.com, where you can sign up for my newsletter and keep up with what I'm writing. I often post photos from my small town in Idaho on my Jenna Night Facebook page, so come visit me there if you'd like.

Kind Regards,
Jenna Night